SPOOKY SOJOURN

ASHLEY LADD

Spooky Sojourn
ISBN # 978-1-78430-274-0
©Copyright Ashley Ladd 2014
Cover Art by Posh Gosh ©Copyright October 2014
Interior text design by Claire Siemaszkiewicz
Totally Bound Publishing

SPOOKY SOJOURN

Dedication

I'd like to thank my husband, David, for being so supportive and loving as we approach our thirty-fifth wedding anniversary, five children, two grandchildren and six fur babies later. Love you, babe!

Chapter One

"Ghosts, schmosts. There's no such thing." Deanna Thompson, the just hired manager of The Gilroy Resort in Homestead, Florida, squared her shoulders and looked around her new abode as she addressed her assistant supervisor, Chantale Veilleux. Not only would she administer the old, luxurious *haunted* hotel, but she would also live on the premises. If she was wrong, she might wind up as crazy as the last manager who had run out of the building in his skivvies, screaming about specters and demons and all kinds of weird shit.

Although she'd worked her way up from the concierge desk attendant to assistant manager to general manager of smaller motels and establishments, this was the first time Deanna had supervised a resort-size hotel. It was also the first time she'd supervised a haunted inn—not that she or the owners believed in ghosts. In fact, the owners demanded that she put a high priority on proving that the lodge wasn't haunted. More and more guests, as well as staff, were reporting spirit sightings and refusing to return until the place had been exorcised.

Chantale, a five foot tall, short-haired, soft-spoken Haitian American with graying hair cropped close to her head squinted her already small eyes. Her lashes glinted with sparkly, silvery mascara that made them look more extraordinary than they might otherwise be. She motioned the sign of the cross over her chest and whispered back as if aghast, "Don't let *them* hear you. They won't be happy."

"Them? You mean the ghosts? You really believe in them?" Unable to comprehend what she'd just heard, Deanna lowered her voice, hoping she didn't sound as incredulous as she felt. There was no need to antagonize her new coworker. Still, she shook her head inwardly that her assistant believed the madcap stories.

Chantale nodded, and she bounced her gaze around the room as though she was seeking something that frightened her. "*Oui.* They are genuine. Everyone on our staff, including me, knows about Mademoiselle Lynette and Monsieur Grant. If you had grown up in Haiti like I did, you'd know ghosts and voodoo are very real. They're not to be messed with."

"Then why do you remain here?" Perplexed, Deanna needed to know. She watched her assistant very carefully for nonverbal clues.

"Mademoiselle and Monsieur don't mean us harm. They want exoneration. They can't rest until they get it. I want to help them." Chantale made wide gestures with her hands in the air like she was painting an invisible picture which made her ample chest rise and fall quickly as if she had trouble breathing.

Needing answers she pressed harder. "But so many of our staff have quit. Are those who remain scared of the ghosts? Or do they feel like you do?"

"It's a mixture. But most are frightened." Chantale's right eye began to tic.

Deanna narrowed her eyes at her new acquaintance. Her heart raced. Her toes curled. She didn't want her staff distracted by such nonsense. In particular, she didn't want anyone else to quit, particularly not her assistant manager. The owners were already horrified with the attrition rate so she had to fix this mess — whatever it was. "What do they do? I mean, how do the ghosts make their presence known? Has anyone actually seen them?"

Shrugging, Chantale held out her hands, palms up. "No one has seen the ghosts but there are very strange goings-on. They like to bowl. Pins, in particular entire strikes, fall without anything touching them, especially after hours when the lanes are closed. Sometimes pins start flying around in the bowling alley, chasing our attendants. In the kitchen, gourmet dishes are cooked that nobody admits to preparing, often with food we didn't have on hand. Sometimes butcher knives fly around the kitchen too. It is said that Monsieur was quite the pro bowler and that Mademoiselle was an aspiring chef."

Really? Flying bowling pins? Butcher knives? Horrible visions of the latter flying around the kitchen filled Deanna's mind and she shivered. What if it was true? But it couldn't be true! She had to be the voice of reason around her so she asked, "Has anybody installed video cameras to see what's *really* going on? To catch the mystery bowlers and chefs?"

"*Oui, Mademoiselle…*"

"Please call me Deanna."

"Deanna," Chantale said in her soft, French Creole accent. "The video cameras haven't captured any ghosts. They only show the mysterious events."

"Do you have time now to show me around the hotel?" Deanna asked her second in command curiously.

An infectious grin spread across Chantale's attractive face and her cheeks dimpled. "But of course. I would be delighted."

Deanna learned a lot as Chantale led her throughout the three-building resort consisting of fifteen hundred rooms. Built a few years before the turn of the twentieth century, the resort provided four-star accommodation and a family-friendly atmosphere that lured guests back year after year. There was plenty of history too, including stories of big-time mobsters who had liked to hide out here when things got too hot in Miami back in the thirties and forties, and a modern day Romeo and Juliet who had either committed suicide or had been murdered in the seventies. Stunning, the lobby in the main structure's concierge area was a palatial mixture of white marble columns and floors with gold filigree ceilings. Potted palm trees and large flower bouquets added spots of vibrant color.

Stained-glass windows and plush white carpets decorated the luxury spa on the second level of the first building. Next door was a highly sought after unisex hair salon. Guests and locals alike kept the spa and salon booked. Nearby, several banquet areas filled the rest of the second story. They examined three additional floors of hotel rooms topping the business-filled second floor.

Neon lights and scads of slot machines lined the casino on the first floor of the second building.

Thunderous booms burst out of the bowling alley that housed a big portion of the bottom section beside the casino. A children's play area sprawled across half the first floor area of the third building, allowing parents a brief respite from their kids.

Finally, a ballroom, specialty gift shops, and more banquet rooms populated the third and last edifice.

Awed, Deanna wondered if she was up to managing such a huge hotel, haunted or not.

"Let me show you the grounds. We'll hitch a ride." Chantale got out her cell phone and clicked an icon. Rapidly, she spoke in Spanish to the person on the other end of the line.

After Deanna pulled her sunglasses out of her pocket and put them on, they walked to the back grounds. Within moments, a middle-aged Hispanic man drove up with a white golf cart and they climbed into the back seat and took a tour of two large outdoor swimming pools, a golf course, gorgeous gardens and an impressive equestrian center.

The grounds were wondrous, well kept and attractive. If she were a ghost, she'd never want to leave this home. "This is amazing. I'm honored I was selected to manage this place."

Squinting against the sun, Chantale shook her head. Deep lines etched her forehead and she frowned. "I wouldn't feel honored yet. Things could get very dangerous. This is a serious matter, not to be taken lightly."

With assurance, Deanna believed that. She just didn't trust that ghosts had anything to do with any of this and she planned to prove it. If she were a betting woman, she'd wager that someone was out to shut down the resort.

* * * *

Once they had finished checking out the grounds, Deanna was ready to meet the staff. "Can you introduce me to the employees on duty?"

"*Mais oui, madem—* Deanna. My pleasure. I must prepare you that we have a colorful cast of personalities. Of course, the normal people were scared off by the poltergeists." Chantale led her through the maze of hallways back to the lobby and the concierge desk.

A plump young woman with a midnight-blue Mohawk and at least six earrings in each ear manned the desk. A living lightning rod, she wore several gold chains around her neck and arms and a gold nose stud. Rings adorned every finger, even her thumbs. Her nails were painted nicely but they were at least an inch long. She sat reading a book and looked annoyed that she'd been interrupted. Chantale whispered in an aside that the woman was Brenna and that her coworker was Teena.

The other woman called Teena looked to be in her early forties. Tattoos covered her from her wrists to her neck. She wore her long pink hair loose around her scrawny shoulders.

Unable to stop herself, Deanna had to ask, "Isn't there a dress code?"

"*Oui*, but Juan, our former manager, didn't enforce it. As I said, it's difficult to get people to work for us. It's even more complicated to get them to stay." The assistant manager led her over to the concierges and introduced her.

Next, they visited the kitchen and met the head chef José, and his sous chefs Frankie, Tessa and Sebastiao. Bald, José sported a tattoo of a cobra on the back of his head. Horns sprouted from his forehead. A gay black man in his early forties, Frankie waved his hands around a lot. Long, light brown dreadlocks that reminded Deanna of Medusa sprouted from Tessa's head. Sebastiao was Hispanic with a bald head and a long handlebar mustache with not merely one handlebar, but four on each side. Gold decorated several of his teeth.

Uncomfortable with the devil-horned chef, Deanna itched to get away from the kitchen's supervisor. She hoped that he stayed in the kitchen so the guests never saw the guy. She was sure they'd prefer the ghosts to him. "I'd like to meet with our head of security and get his take on the haunting situation."

"You mean *her*. Her name is Emily Spencer and she has a staff of five."

Chantale's soft slippers created sucking noises on the marble floors as they made their way to the security office.

A few moments later, Chantale led her into the safety office.

Deanna smiled up at the six foot tall, balding woman with wispy, fading red hair. "Emily, meet our new manager, Deanna Thompson."

Deanna stuck her hand out and shook Emily's. The woman's firm, no-nonsense grip impressed Deanna. "Nice to meet you. Do you have a few minutes so we can discuss the ghost issue? I need to know more about it."

Harrumphing, the officer turned on her high heels and entered a large office. She motioned for them to sit across from her chair then closed the door. After she took her seat, she shuffled some papers to the side of her desk so she could rest her hands in front of her.

"I'll be blunt. Something's going on, but our security cameras haven't been able to catch the culprits."

Latching on to the fact that Emily didn't say *ghosts,* Deanna asked, "So you think someone or several people are perpetrating this ghost ruse?"

Shaking her head, Emily said, "Yes. I don't believe in the supernatural. However, as I explained, we haven't been able to find a credible explanation."

"Do you think someone is trying to put the resort out of business? Does somebody have a tiff against the owners?" Deanna removed a tiny notepad from her shirt pocket and readied herself to jot down notes.

Frowning, Chantale put out her hands. "You Americans refuse to believe the truth. If you can't see something, it must be a fraud or make-believe. I've been telling you that the ghosts are real, that they can't leave here until we help them to move on. We must solve the murders before they can progress."

Stopping herself in mid eye-roll, Emily glared at Chantale. "We don't believe in them because they're myths."

Glad she'd found somebody on her side, Deanna favored the guard with a smile. "Where do we go from here?"

"We hire a paranormal expert. There's a good one out of Miami named Harry DeVeaux." Emily wrote down his information, tore it off her pad of paper then handed it to Deanna.

Confused, Deanna studied it. Then she peered at the redhead. "But you said you don't believe in ghosts. Aren't paranormal experts scam artists?"

Emily rubbed her chin thoughtfully. "He'll disprove the ghost theory. He's done it before."

Narrowing her eyes and thrusting out her chin, Chantale regarded Emily. "And he has proven many times that there *are* ghosts."

"So he says. The fact that he sometimes says there are ghosts will make our clientele and employees believe his findings."

"What if he says there are ghosts? Do we call a priest to have an exorcism? Sprinkle holy water around the hotel?" Sarcasm dripped from Deanna's lips.

"I don't believe you two. You'll incur the specters' wrath. I want no part of this. And for your information, I do sprinkle holy water around at least once a week." Chantale put her fingers in the sign of a cross, rose and, muttering in Creole, backed out of the office.

Disbelieving, Deanna watched her subordinate slink away. She jerked her thumb in the woman's direction. Her heart falling to her knees, she asked, "Is she always like that?"

"Yes, she believes in all that mystical hoo-ha. If she ran the hotel, we'd have ghost tours and séances. In fact, she's proposed we do just that."

How was she going to run this large resort with Chantale as second in command? She wasn't sure of the wisdom in hiring a paranormal investigator when she didn't believe in the psychic shit. Then again, security hadn't been able to prove anything or stop the garbage.

Chapter Two

Vampires, witches and demons took over the hotel that night as a bevy of romance writers went crazy in the hallways and the hotel's largest banquet hall where they held a vampire ball.

Deanna made sure they were fed on time and supplied with a steady flow of wine and liquor. She also oversaw that dirty dishes and glasses were promptly removed.

Hoots and hollers went up from the tipsy authors and their fans when cover models danced and gyrated on the stage, distracting her. Half-naked firemen, astronauts, football players, cowboys and policemen strutted around the room, picked lucky women and swayed with them to slow, sexy music.

Several women who weren't picked danced with other women or in groups.

Some became so drunk that they stumbled around and mangled their words as they sloshed their drinks.

Deanna couldn't wait until a new head of housekeeping and a new headwaiter were hired. The previous ones had walked with the former manager.

Rather, stories said they had run out predicting Armageddon.

A rainy night outside, thunder boomed then the lights went out and the music died. Women screamed. *Damn!*

Then the generator hummed to life and lights flickered on. Relieved, Deanna sighed.

The head of the romance convention approached her. Large warts hung off a pointy nose and a pointy chin on the woman's green face as her beady eyes regarded Deanna curiously. "I'd like to arrange a ghost tour for our conventioneers. How do we go about it?"

Trying not to gulp or turn green herself, Deanna's heart flipped over in her chest. Unhappy about the question, she tried to field it with as much aplomb as possible. "I'm sorry, we don't have ghosts."

The woman's coffee-brown eyes widened with anger. "But your resort is famous for being haunted. We chose your hotel because of it. Do you mean to tell us we were misled? I think you owe us a refund."

Not wishing to offend or anger the guest and unwilling to issue a refund, she stood tall and said, "We do not advertise that we have ghosts or that our establishment is haunted. It has never been proven that there is anything unusual about this hotel."

"It is a well-known fact that this resort is haunted. You need to rethink your stance. We will not be coming back and you will hear from our attorney." With that, the witch stomped off, her high-heeled boots click-clacking on the floor.

Exhaustion claimed Deanna and it was all she could do not to wilt. Double shifts were the worst.

Around two a.m. the party finally wound down, and Deanna helped her waiters clean up as they shooed the night creatures back to their lairs.

As one of the demons headed out, she paused, slapped her hand over her mouth then vomited onto the floor.

The stench made Deanna's stomach roil as she tried not to show emotion.

* * * *

Making a wish list the next day, Deanna added a director of human resources and a head of housekeeping. After dispelling the ghosts hearsay, these particular employees were at the top of her list to hire.

She called the local newspapers and placed several employment ads. She also dialed several employment agencies. To her dismay, several refused to take her business, as they were familiar with the gossip.

"Seriously?" she asked one of them. "You believe this nonsense? There are no such things as ghosts."

"Prove it. Then we'll send applicants, but not until then." The woman slammed the phone down in her ear.

Fed up, Deanna took Harry DeVeaux's number out of her purse and dialed. She half hoped he wouldn't answer, that he would prove to be a flake.

"Harry DeVeaux Paranormal Investigations. Harry speaking," an extremely sexy, deep, masculine voice said.

Taken aback, Deanna almost dropped the receiver. Her spine tingled and her heart threatened to melt. She hadn't expected to have this reaction to the man. Regrouping her composure as best she could, she tried to sound professional. "This is Deanna Thompson, general manager of The Gilroy Resort and Hotel in Homestead, Florida. I'd like to consult with you about engaging your services." Her voice came out breathier, huskier than she'd intended and she bit her trembling lip. *Damn.*

"What would you like to know?"

"Do you charge a fee to disprove there are ghosts in a hotel? Do you have packages? What do they cost?" Nervous, she curled her hair around her finger.

"What makes you so sure we'll dispel the haunted hotel theory? We might prove there are specters in your hotel." His voice had shifted from a friendly professional tone to a cold and chilly one.

"You honestly believe spirits exist? Have you personally seen them? Spoken to them?" Unable to stop herself, she rolled her eyes.

"I take it you don't. So why call me? If I say I believe in ghosts I'm a kook in your book, right?"

She had trouble denying it but realized she was on the verge of losing him. *Way to go. How to win friends and influence people.* "Are you familiar with our hotel? We're losing guests and staff because of alleged poltergeist sightings. I would like you to disprove them."

"What if I prove them? Are you willing to live with my findings whichever direction they fall?"

"Are your methods above board?"

"Do you doubt my professionalism? Are you calling me a fraud?" Incredulity rang in Harry's words.

Unfortunately, the man's voice was deep and dreamy and urged the butterflies in her stomach to twirl unabashedly. Hardly able to believe that she was having this conversation, much less that she was having such a reaction to a person she'd just talked with over the phone, she scratched her head. "I'm not trying to call you anything. I don't believe in the paranormal. I believe there has to be a rational explanation. Someone must be perpetrating a scam on the hotel."

"Perhaps. Or perhaps there are spirits that have been trapped in your abode. You need to open your mind and do some research."

Research? As in read ghost stories? "How much do you charge?"

"That depends how big the job is. How long it takes. It's impossible to tell you over the phone. I'll need to bring my crew to your hotel and make an estimate. Is tomorrow afternoon a good time?"

Wanting the negative buzz stopped now she pressed, "The sooner the better. You can't come this afternoon?"

"Tomorrow afternoon is the soonest we can make it."

She hoped he would be as tough doing his job as he had been on her. She also prayed he worked quickly and cheaply.

"Gather any proof you have and show me tomorrow. The more evidence, the better."

"Certainly." Hopefully her staff had kept accurate records. She made a note to see Emily Spencer when she ended the phone call.

"Is one p.m. good?"

"Do you know where we are located?" She wondered what he looked like. DeVeaux sounded French. Was he tall, blond and blue-eyed? Or was he short, ebony-eyed and well built? Maybe he was a redhead with a face full of freckles with emerald-green eyes. Was he a charmer when he wasn't annoyed?

"Yep. I've pulled you up on my map and I have a good GPS. Don't worry. We'll be there. Just be sure to open your mind to the possibilities."

"Uh. Okay." Oh, her mind was opening to possibilities. Just not to ghosts. Unsure that she could change her mind so fast about spirits, she was afraid she was lying to the man. But she needed professional proof on her side. Unfortunately, she wondered if most people would believe Harry's findings. Then she remembered that way too many guests were boycotting the hotel because they believed it was haunted. She had to shake her head. What was wrong with everyone?

A glutton for punishment, Deanna stuck around for another double shift. Not only was the hotel short-staffed, and wild romance writers and readers were running amok, but she wanted to check out the ghost reports. Hoping those responsible for the odd sightings would be active tonight, she thought she'd check out the bowling alley and kitchen after hours with her trusty webcam.

First, she stopped at Emily Spencer's office and made copies of the ghost 'evidence', including information about Lynette Cambridge, Grant Haynes and Lynette's stepsister Roxanne Cambridge-Anderson, now a rich and powerful Miami socialite.

Reading the file as she walked away from the office, she chewed her lip. There had been speculation that Roxanne Cambridge had somehow been involved in the deaths although the allegations had never been proven. Would there be any point in trying to prove the woman's culpability now?

* * * *

A few hours later in the bowling alley, Deanna gathered pillows and blankets and spread them out on one of the seats. She also took the ghost files and her computer complete with her webcam. If something funky was going on inside she was determined to video tape it.

Wide awake, she ambled around the lanes, looking for any sign of movement, anything out of the ordinary. Fortunately — or unfortunately — everything looked to be in place.

After a couple of rounds about the area, and unwilling to give up on her mission, she settled in with her computer. She couldn't get Harry DeVeaux's voice out of her mind. Not understanding her fixation, she wanted to purge him from her mind. She hadn't had such a reaction to a man in ages, and *never* over just a voice. For heaven's sake, she hadn't even seen the man. She had no idea how old he was, so he could be eighty and he could be three feet tall and have a face full of moles.

However, she didn't think so. His voice was too sensual, too sexy, even when he was clearly annoyed. Her sixth sense told her he was tall, dark, handsome and around her age.

Cheering and laughter rose from a nearby banquet hall, and she remembered the romance writers. She wondered how hard it would be to write a romance. It must be fun to live vicariously through a heroine, to make up a sexy hero and fall in love with him. Could she do it? And what about the sex scenes?

Heat rose in her neck and bloomed into her cheeks. She was glad no one was around to see her. Unless the ghosts were watching…

She had to laugh aloud at her derision. Of course, the ghosts weren't watching, because there weren't any such things. But she was going to stay the night to prove their nonexistence. Another evening, she would hide video cameras around in case there were real people pulling pranks and in case they had rigged the hotel's video cameras.

Obsessed with the paranormal investigator, intrigued by the romance writers, she opened her computer. As if some force guided her fingers beyond her reckoning, she opened a free blog, made up the pseudonym Thomasina Deanngelo and started writing her fantasy starring herself and Harry DeVeaux.

New to the greater Miami area, a closet nudist, I had to visit the famous nude beach. Still, I didn't want anyone to know who I was, so I took care to wear dark glasses, tie my hair up and hide it under a baseball cap. I wore dark, nondescript clothing, ditched my car about three blocks from the beach and trekked the rest of the way. Once there, I froze.

Scads of people populated the beach. Some were completely dressed. Then some were topless. Finally, several were completely nude except for flip-flops.

Now that I was here, I wasn't sure I could shed my top much less all my clothing. What if someone recognized me?

But that was silly. I'd only recently moved here. Barely anybody knew me. Plus, my face was hidden.

After coming all this way, I'd call myself all kinds of a coward if I chickened out now.

Inhaling deeply, I gathered my resolve. Then I lifted my shirt off, pushed down my pants, folded them and put them in my backpack. Left in only my bikini, I soaked in the sun as I rubbed sunscreen SPF 30 onto my lily-white flesh. I definitely wasn't a bronzed Floridian, not yet at least. Soon.

As I procrastinated, I wondered if I was truly a nudist. Then I just did it. I reached back and unhooked my bikini top then tossed it up into the air. Feeling freer than I ever had, I laughed, a clear, tinkling sound from deep in my throat. Wanting to feel freer yet, I stood and wiggled out of my bikini bottoms. I was so glad I'd had a Brazilian wax job, that I didn't have a big, ugly bush between my legs. I was also glad I had a slender but not too thin body. I don't think I'd go sans clothing if I had excess rolls on my tummy. Unfortunately, that didn't stop some of my fellow nudists.

Then I saw him – a living god.

A halo of light seemed to follow him. He was taller than the other men, at least six foot three. He had springy, soft mahogany brown hair, brilliant blue eyes, and a sensual mouth. He was muscular but not overpoweringly so. His broad chest tapered down to slim hips and an oh-my-God gorgeously long, thick cock. And he was staring at me.

More unbelievably, his penis started to grow longer, wider as he regarded me with a beckoning smile. Then he crooked his finger at me. At least I think he was motioning to me.

Unsure, I pointed at myself.

When he nodded, I almost sank into the sand. Butterflies pirouetted in my stomach in a not so elegant ballet. Nervous wrecks like me, they collided into each other then fell to the base of my stomach. My ankles went weak and threatened to buckle under me. I longed to walk into his embrace then stroll off into the sunset with him and make mad, passionate love right here on this beach in front of all and sundry. Who knew I had exhibitionist tendencies as well?

Then again, what if he was the most beautiful serial killer on Earth? Ted Bundy was an attractive man.

Oh, shut up, inner voice. If I wanted to play it safe, I wouldn't be standing completely nude on a beach in front of hundreds of people. So I let him reel me in.

Slowly, sensually, I sashayed over to my would-be lover. At least I hoped he would be. I'd never made love to a stranger before, but then again, today was a day of firsts.

"Hi," I said oh so brilliantly and coquettishly. I wondered what had happened to my vocabulary. I wasn't normally so shy.

"Hi, gorgeous. What's a girl like you doing on a beach like this?"

"Ha ha. Soaking in some Florida sunshine." Hoping to meet a hottie like you. Hoping to get fucked by a hottie like you.

Surprised by my errant thoughts, I was suffused with heat and I was sure I was turning bright, cherry red. Did that mean my breasts would turn crimson too? That reminded me that I hadn't protected my pussy or my breasts with sunscreen yet. I'd been – er – distracted by Mr Hottie.

"Is something wrong?"

Blinking, I looked up at him. Should I be honest or coy? Finally, I decided to be honest. I held up the bottle of sunscreen. "I just remembered I forgot to put my sunscreen on my breasts and my, uh…" I couldn't say pussy to someone I'd just met.

"Beautiful pussy. I'd be delighted to help. It's one of my specialties."

I was almost disappointed but what did I expect? That this was his virgin voyage on the nudist beach like me?

"Okay." I handed over the sunscreen.

Mr Hottie threaded his fingers through mine and led me to a semi private spot on the beach, behind a large outcropping of rocks where a couple of beach towels had been laid out. He instructed me to stand in the middle.

Then he closed the gap between us. Huskily, he drawled beside my ear so close his hot breath tickled my skin, "Are you ready? Are you sure it's okay I touch you? That I rub this all over your luscious body?"

"It's fine. Please rub it on me. You'll be doing me a huge favor." It was so much more than okay. I couldn't wait to feel his hands explore my body, to rub the cream onto my breasts, around my pussy, onto my clitoris... And I can't wait to return the favor and rub it all over you.

He held out his hand and wiggled his fingers. "Here. Give it to me." He took it, poured some in his hands and started rubbing it onto me. Not at all shy, he slathered it onto my breasts, taking his time tweaking my nipples, elongating them.

A slow burn started in my nipples and licked throughout my veins. The heat flushed through me and I trembled under his ministrations. Hussy that I am, I wanted so much more. I wanted his cock inside me, fucking me wildly, in front of this beach of sunbathers. Not only am I a hussy but an exhibitionist. He worked his way down the slope of my breasts, to my belly, to my pussy. He insinuated his hand between my legs and I opened them wider to give him better access. God, but I yearned to have him inside me.

Unable to stop myself, I pleaded, "Fuck me. Here. Now."

"I don't even know your name."

I held out my hand to shake his. "I'm Thomasina."

He took mine and shook it. "I'm Harry."

"Nice to meet you, Harry. Fuck me now. Right here. Please!" I was so hot I was about to spontaneously combust.

Miraculously, he pulled a condom out of mid-air and handed it to me. I slid it onto his gloriously long cock – all nine or ten inches of it. I hope I can take all of him. I sure as hell am going to try.

Chuckling, he scooped me off my feet and deposited me onto his beach towel. Then he lowered himself on top of me, slowly, inexorably, until he was a hair's breadth from my lips, until his cock was teasing my pussy.

"Are you sure you want this?" he questioned.

My scalp prickled. My fingers itched. My toes curled. "I've never been surer of anything. I want you here and now."

"Okay, pretty lady. I am here to please you." With one smooth, graceful thrust, he plunged into me.

He was so long, so thick that I screamed in ecstasy as I lifted my hips to meet him and squeezed him tightly. We moved together in an erotic rhythm. I was so turned on, knowing others were watching, knowing I was being fucked by a complete stranger, that my world shattered into a billion kaleidoscope pieces and I came long, hard and way too quickly.

As if he's on my wavelength, mere moments later, he shuddered against me, his fingers biting into my arms and he came too. Romantically, he feathered kisses along my jaw to my lips.

Wow!

Deanna re-read her fantasy, barely able to believe that she'd penned it, wondering if she should delete it. Did she really want to make out with Harry, a perfect stranger, on a public beach? Did she really want her words on the Internet, even in a supposedly private blog under a make-believe name?

Well, it was confidential, right? As long as she didn't give anybody the web address or password or tell them about it, it would remain secret.

Enough fantasizing! She had to get back to work. Dragging the files out, she familiarized herself with the ghost sightings as well as Lynette and Grant's history. By the time she was finished, she knew how they'd died and the theories about their suicides-slash-murders. She also knew that everybody was afraid to point fingers at the now very influential and powerful Roxanne Cambridge-Anderson. Could Roxanne be behind the haunting nonsense? Did she want the hotel shut down? But that made no sense. The rumors portrayed Roxanne as a murderess. It wouldn't be in her best interest to keep their legend alive.

Deanna's temples began to ache the harder she thought about everything, so she decided to go to sleep. Hopefully she'd awake if any hijinks took place in the bowling alley.

* * * *

About three a.m. deafening booms awoke her. Light brightened lane fourteen and all but one pin lay scattered on the wooden floor.

Groggy, Deanna tried to gather her senses. She looked around then, to her horror, she saw an iridescent figure of a man on lane fourteen picking up a glowing ball. Collecting her presence of mind, she grabbed her webcam, pointed it at the ghostly shape and turned it on. Shaking, she tried to hold her computer steady. Not believing what she was seeing, she knew there had to be a rational explanation. Perhaps some machine was projecting the image onto the lanes. Perhaps a real person stood in front of her in glowing phosphorescent powder.

Whatever or whoever it was picked up the ball, and knocked down the spare pin. Then the 'apparition' bowled three strikes in a row.

Unexpectedly, he turned and glared at her, fire shooting from his eyes. Pins flew from all the lanes at her. Her heart racing, she ducked under the score table.

Flummoxed, she checked her webcam to ensure that it had recorded everything.

Finally, the pins returned to their positions and the man shimmered away into a billion tiny sparkles of light. Shaking, Deanna picked up her computer, abandoning everything else, and rushed back to the sanctuary of her room.

What in the hell is happening?

Chapter Three

One always to do his research, Harry Googled The Gilroy Hotel and Resort. He also looked up Deanna Thompson, the general manager. He liked to know who he was dealing with.

As he'd figured, there was a lot of paranormal history about The Gilroy. It sounded like the typical haunted hotel. Lots of people died in hotels—suicides, murders, heart attacks. Why shouldn't a ghost or two get stuck sometimes?

The sad, romantic Romeo and Juliet story of Lynette Cambridge and her fiancé Grant Haynes drew his attention. In particular, the fact that Lynette's wicked stepsister was *the* famous and all-powerful Miami socialite Roxanne Cambridge-Anderson made him sit up taller in his chair. Something smelled fishy about the story. Some people thought she had killed them because she was in love with Grant and couldn't stand to be a thwarted lover. Others said that she had wanted the family inheritance. Some said both. One thing was for sure—she was filthy rich now and she would never have been if her stepsister had lived.

Another thing was certain—it would be suicide to tangle with the woman.

He leaned back in his chair, disliking this development, not that he was a policeman who would have to face her down. Still, she may not like him poking into her business, even on this level. Then again, did he concern himself with politics? No, but it was always good to know what and who he was dealing with.

The ghosts Lynette and Grant—she an aspiring chef and he a pro bowler—seemed like nice enough people in life. Apparently, they had kept their proclivities. At least he doubted there were other bowling ghosts in the same hotel. In fact, he hadn't run into another bowling ghost anywhere. This assignment might prove interesting.

Curious about the woman who had hired his company, he looked her up. When he found a picture of a lush brunette with milk-chocolate-brown eyes and luscious, perky lips, he sucked in a breath. *Wow!* She was a beauty. Divorced once in her twenties, no children, and she hadn't remarried. Instead, now that she was in her late thirties, she'd pursued her career and had advanced to hotel management.

After several hours of diligent researching for everything ever written about the manager, for every sordid secret she might be hiding, he found a newly created private blog with the hotel's IP address that piqued his curiosity. A world-class hacker, he couldn't rest until he'd cracked it open. Obviously, Thomasina Deanngelo was Deanna Thompson. When he read the entry, he almost swallowed his tongue. Why had she named the hero Harry? They'd never met, so it had to be coincidence. Didn't it?

Still, he had to wonder if it really was a fluke. And why so erotic? His cock swelled and he started having fantasies of his own. Suddenly, he wanted to meet this woman. He hoped he could keep things on a professional level today. If he remembered what a disbeliever she was, what a closed mind she kept, he should be able to do so. But why did she have to be so attractive? On the outside, he reminded himself. Not on the inside.

But one p.m. couldn't come fast enough. He itched to reach the hotel and meet Deanna Thompson in person. To fill the time, he gathered his equipment, checked with his assistants and filled his gas tank. He took a second shower, shaved and splashed on cologne. He looked himself in the face and wondered why he was so nervous to meet this client. He'd never been apprehensive to meet a customer before. Of course, he'd never had a client fantasize about him—that he knew of.

After he'd dressed—more carefully than normal to look nice—he drove to the office, picked up his associate Bruno then headed south toward Homestead to the resort. South Miami traffic was lighter than usual at this time of day and they made good time.

When he walked up to the resort, the art deco design on the front of the main building impressed him. Stained glass, mirrors, chrome and inlaid wood decorated the façade. It was not romantic or fussy, but rather what someone of the 1920s had thought the future would look like.

Beside him, Bruno, a big muscular guy with a Vandyke, wheeled their monitoring equipment to the door. Harry had invested in expensive, modern gear so that he would beat his competitors. They passed a bevy of women scurrying out of the door, followed by a man in a chef's uniform with horns sprouting from his forehead that looked implanted, not merely glue-ons.

Harry blinked and did a double take at the weird dude. Once inside, he took inventory of the marble columns and floors and the gold filigree ceilings. He wondered where he'd find the sexy manager and if she'd still be as prickly as she'd been on the phone. Spying the concierge desk, he made a beeline for it, bemused that one attendant had a blue Mohawk and the other had long pink hair and wore a dog collar with spikes. What kind of hotel were they running?

Trying to be charming, he smiled and leaned on the desk. "Where might I find your general manager Deanna Thompson? I'm Harry DeVeaux and I have a one p.m. appointment with her."

Determined footsteps clicked on the marble floor and stopped behind him. "Mr DeVeaux?"

He turned on his boot heel and his gaze fell on a woman more beautiful and regal than her photograph. Taken off guard, imagining her naked on a Miami beach, his mouth went dry, he swallowed hard and he struggled to keep his expression neutral. This was the beauty who was fantasizing about him? The one who had views diametrically opposed to his?

Bruno elbowed him and cleared his throat. Under his breath he uttered, "Shake her hand. Say something, man."

Feeling like a douche, still unable to get the vision of her naked out of his head, Harry stuck out his hand. "Nice to meet you, Ms Thompson. I'm Harry DeVeaux. This is my assistant Bruno O'Conner."

"Likewise. Please join me in my office. I want to show you something." She thrust her chin out and led the way, her head held high. Her dark coffee-colored hair tickled the small of her back. Although her tresses were long, they cascaded into a gorgeous silken waterfall that he longed to sift his fingers through. Below her hair, her hips curved outward from her slim waist. He'd bet she didn't have an ounce of flab on her frame.

Almost on autopilot, he followed her as Bruno gave him odd looks. He didn't know how he could be so attracted to a woman's veneer when he'd been so annoyed when conversing with her. Never had he had such a conflicting reaction to anyone. Her blog wasn't helping, either.

When they reached a large office with a wall of windows on the far side overlooking the pool and golf course and part of the parking lot, he walked inside behind her, stood by a seat across from the desk and waited for her to sit before he did. Then he folded himself into the chair and crossed his leg over the other. He rested his hands in his lap and regarded his would-be client.

"Did you do your research?" he questioned politely.

She nodded. The sunlight filtering in through the window bounced off the highlights in her hair as she opened a laptop. "I did. I read up on our hotel history, especially about our famous spirit residents Lynette Cambridge and Grant Haynes. My assistant manager is under the impression that they want our help to solve their murders so they can leave in peace."

Absorbing this, Harry tapped his fingers against his leg. He'd found this same information and concurred with her assistant manager. "Do you agree with her?"

"Do you mean do I suddenly believe in ghosts?" She shook her head, clicked some keys on the computer then turned the screen around. She stabbed the enter key. "I don't think so, but watch this. There has to be some explanation."

He pinned his gaze to the monitor and watched the glowing figure of a young man then some pins—not just one or two, but hundreds—floating around the lanes.

Lifting his eyes to meet hers he asked, "When did this happen? Who took the video?"

She stopped chewing her bottom lip. "Last night, about three a.m. I spent the night in the bowling alley with my webcam and I captured this on film. What do you think?"

Scrubbing his hand over his freshly shaven chin, he leaned closer to the video. "You saw this with your own eyes and you filmed it and yet you still don't believe in ghosts?"

Splaying her hands before her, her eyes troubled, she said, "I don't know what the hell to believe. I don't discount that somebody wants to hurt The Gilroy. That's why I'd like your company to check things out for us. Will you do this? Can you give me an estimate?"

"Will you keep an open mind? It won't be cheap. We have sophisticated equipment, plus we have to set up shop for several nights in numerous areas of the hotel. We'd like to situate our own surveillance equipment in the kitchen, the bowling alley, and the hotel rooms where the sightings have been reported."

When she wrung her hands, he knew she wasn't as cool and collected as she pretended.

"Okay," she said, "I'd like to see the estimate. How soon can you get it to me?"

He'd already worked it up when he'd done his research on the place, so he pulled it out of his briefcase. He slid it across the desk to her. "Here it is.

I'll be here with my crew to supervise. I'd also like to interview the staff, especially your assistant manager, head of security, anybody who's witnessed the ghost sightings and the staff that have worked here for any length of time. Is that acceptable? Do you have an empty office we can use?"

"The one next to mine is available. You may use that. How soon can you start?"

Eager to be so close to her, he met and held her gaze. "Will tomorrow be soon enough?"

* * * *

Well aware that there were sharp knives in the kitchen, Deanna decided to spend the night there anyway. Once again, she'd brought her webcam.

"Okay, Lynette, or whoever has been burning the midnight cooking oil in here, you can come out. I only want what's best for all of us." Or did she? She and the owners wanted the ghosts—or whoever was scaring away the guests—gone. But if there truly was such a thing as spirits, and they were nice ones—not frightening evil-type demons—then she hoped they went to heaven or wherever good people were supposed to go after they died. She was sure that wasn't The Gilroy Hotel and Resort. At least she wouldn't want to be stuck here for eternity.

She sauntered around the gourmet kitchen with the industrial-sized refrigerators, ovens and the prep areas. Since she'd been told that different food would show up from what was available in the kitchen, she took inventory. It gave her something to do while she waited. Besides, she wondered if she would find demons hissing in the refrigerator or if eggs would start jumping out of their carton and sizzle on the countertops. She had to chuckle at her sarcasm, although it did feel as if she was hiring the Ghostbusters. Isn't that essentially what Harry's company was—just a rose by any other name?

Remembering how the bowling pins had flown at her, she flinched. There weren't as many knives in the kitchen as pins in the alley, but one blade could be deadly.

"You're not going to hurt me, are you, Lynette? Grant didn't want to hurt me last night, either, did he? He just wanted to scare me off."

Unfortunately, nobody answered, so she continued to write down items as she spoke aloud, feeling silly talking to herself. "But that makes no sense. Why would you want to scare me off if you want my help? Or maybe you don't think I'm here to help you? Maybe you think I'm the enemy?"

Anchoring her hair behind her ear, she looked up and around just in case there was an apparition nearby. There wasn't, at least not that she could see.

"How can I prove I'm not the enemy? How can I help?"

If her offer to help didn't bring the so-called ghosts out in the open, then it probably was a scam artist trying to hurt the hotel. Or the specters were somewhere else. They weren't omniscient, were they?

Oh, God.

Were Chantale and Harry infecting her? She didn't really believe in spirits, did she?

Unlike the night before, nothing out of the ordinary happened.

* * * *

"Wakie-wakie, Princess Dee Dee," a strange masculine voice said, as if through a fog.

When Deanna opened her eyes, she screamed and scooted backward. Her hand flew to her throat as she focused her eyes on a demon with horns sprouting from his forehead. When her vision cleared and she recognized José, and Frankie, who stared at her wide-eyed with concern, she released a loud sigh as she struggled to her feet. "I'm so sorry. That was unforgivable of me."

"I get it all the time. Why were you sleeping on the kitchen floor? Doesn't the hotel give you a room of your own?" José bent over and gathered her bedding. Frankie helped him fold it.

She pushed her tousled hair away from her eyes. "I was trying to catch the ghosts."

"Did you see them?" José looked around and frowned. "I don't see any dishes. The knives are all in their proper places. Doesn't look like anybody's been cooking."

Shaking her head, Deanna said, "No. Not last night." She didn't share what had happened the previous evening in the bowling alley.

Alarmed that it was time for Harry DeVeaux and his crew to show up, she glanced at her watch. Luckily it was early, only six-thirty a.m. Still, she needed to get a shower, wash her hair, and put her face on before she had to face him—er—them.

* * * *

"Ms Thompson, we need you at the concierge desk immediately. A guest requests your presence," Brenna said breathily as though she was about to hyperventilate.

"I'll be right there." Deanna's still-damp hair, only half blow-dried, hung in disarray about her head and she hadn't had a chance to put on her makeup. She grimaced at herself in the mirror as she hurriedly tied her hair up in a high ponytail. At least no one could tell which half of her hair was curled. She swept a mascara wand over her lashes, jumped into a skirt, yanked up the zipper and threw on a blouse. Then she stepped into heels and sprinted to the lobby.

"Are you the general manager?" a curly-haired, sixtyish, brunette woman shrieked as she ran at Deanna. "I took my husband to the emergency room this morning. He was puking all night after eating at *your* restaurant."

Appalled, hoping it wasn't their restaurant at fault, Deanna straightened her frame and stood tall. "We haven't had any other reports. What did he have to eat?"

"Blackened Tilapia. The hospital said it had to be the fish. What are you going to do about it? You poisoned him!" Fury lit the woman's emerald eyes. She jabbed her finger into Deanna's chest.

The stabs were painful—and personal. Deanna stepped back from her attacker. "I'd like to see a copy of the reports, and *if* the hotel is at fault, we'll certainly compensate you for your expenses."

"And pain and suffering. My son's an attorney and we're going to sue you for all you're worth! You'll be hearing from us. We'll be asking around to find out if anybody else came down ill from your bad chow too. It's inexcusable to serve rancid food."

"Ma'am, we only serve the best fare. Something must have gone horribly wrong with that one dish…"

"Of course something went horribly wrong! My husband almost died. He still might. They admitted him to the hospital with food poisoning. It's your fault."

As manager, the buck stopped at her, so it was *her* responsibility. She prayed that no one else came down with the same symptoms.

A stooped and lanky, seven-foot-tall elderly man with wispy gray hair approached holding his stomach. "I overheard. I had the Tilapia too, and I've been sick all night. I'm on my way to the hospital. It *must* be your food. I hope you'll cover my expenses."

Deanna's heart shriveled. What were the chances now that this wasn't their liability? "Of course we will, if it was our fault. Please bring us the hospital paperwork and if you have it, a copy of last night's restaurant bill."

"I paid with cash and I didn't save the bill. So you're saying you won't take responsibility for your screw-up?" the woman shrilled, her face mottling.

"I'm sure we can work this out." Deanna's head ached and she hoped that no one else had eaten the fish. Within the hour, five more guests who had dined on the Tilapia came down ill. Worse, the upset woman reported it to the press. Reporters swarmed the building, and Deanna suddenly had her own paparazzi.

Finally, after she persuaded the journalists to leave, dreading what they were going to write about the hotel, she met with her second in command and the other managers.

She turned to the head chef. "José, what went wrong with the fish? Why do we have seven guests who were sufficiently ill that they had to visit the emergency room? They all ate the tilapia. Hospital reports are pouring in and the press is on our backs. This is going to be in the headlines today and the owners won't be happy when I tell them."

Spreading his hands wide, the chef looked at her with big puppy-dog eyes. "The fish was fresh. We only use completely sanitary methods to prepare it. It must have come from the manufacturer tainted. That, or the ghosts poisoned it."

Trying to bite back her anger, Deanna pounded her fist on the table, making several of her managers jump back in fear. "I don't want to hear any nonsense that the ghosts did it. We'll look into the possibility that we were sold rotten fish. Don't we have a way to test the fish when we get it?"

"It could have been full of mercury and we couldn't see it. It's happening more and more." José fingered his horns.

"If fish is that much of a hazard, maybe we should take it off the menu." She looked around at her team for their reactions. Some nodded and some frowned. "We'll research this further. Are there any complaints other than the bad fish yesterday?"

"The guest in room three-eleven complained that the maid was impertinent. She refused to leave extra soaps, shampoos and sets of towels. They wanted ten each," Sydney, the temporary head of housekeeping, said. A Jamaican with a strong patois, he was a little difficult to understand.

Astonished at the request, Deanna repeated dumbly, "Ten each? Did they sneak eight extra people into their room? Chantale, can we roll the video cameras in their hallway and look into this? I want to know if they're hiding extra people without paying for them. I also want to know if the maid was rude in any way with her response other than saying no."

"*Oui.* I'll do that as soon as we finish." Chantale jotted down a note on her pad of paper.

"Anything else?" She let her gaze linger for a few seconds each on the rest of her crew, hoping there weren't going to be any more issues for today.

Emily Spencer heaved a large sigh. "The guests in room three-twenty-seven complained to security that their neighbors were noisy and running amok around the hallways all of last night. That unit is near the block of rooms we are renting to the romance writers' convention."

"Do we have any open rooms in a different building away from the romance convention, where we can move the guests in question? Also we should comp them a night. Write that down too," she said to Chantale, tapping the woman's notebook.

"I'll see to it immediately." Scribbling swiftly, Chantale leaned over her paper.

"In the future, we should keep conventions like this contained, if at all possible. Do we have any similar ones booked soon?" Deanna looked at Chantale.

Squinting, her associate pulled out a spreadsheet and smoothed it out in front of her. She stabbed the paper and said, "There's a Star Trek Con in two weeks. They tend to get rowdy. There's also a vampire convention in four weeks. They can be disorderly too. Then there's a large number of high school soccer teams checking in once the romance writers check out."

Sydney raised his hand. "We found bedbugs in several rooms. We have to call the exterminator again."

"*Again*? Has this been a continuing problem? For how long?" She turned to Chantale. She really needed to hire a new head of housekeeping soon to handle all of this.

"Several months. It's been a difficult problem. The last manager was not on top of things. We're glad to have you." Chantale offered her a hopeful smile.

Deanna felt like hanging her head in her hands, but refrained. She had to keep her head held high and a smile in place for her staff. "Do we have a contract with an exterminator? Let me see it as soon as we're done here."

The phone rang. Deanna answered.

Brenna said breathlessly, "We have a problem and need you, Sydney and the civil engineering staff right away."

"What's up?" Deanna said in a low voice.

"A guest got her toe stuck in the bathtub faucet. She's completely nude and totally stuck. She's screaming at the top of her lungs, and according to her roommate, hyperventilating and asthmatic. If we don't get her out soon, she might go into shock."

"We'll be right there." Deanna looked at her squad. "The meeting is adjourned. Sydney. Yaniv. Come with me."

The men stood and followed her.

* * * *

Excitement thrummed in Harry's veins as he entered the hotel with two members of his team. He enjoyed his mission to find ghosts, to help them move on to the next realm. Most spirits had a story and he'd bet the ones haunting The Gilroy were Lynette Cambridge and Grant Haynes. Unless there were other less publicized deaths at the hotel. He'd have to look into that.

He walked up to the girl with the blue Mohawk and gave her his most dazzling smile. He enjoyed it when she melted under his charm. "I'm here to see Deanna Thompson, the general manager. We have an appointment at ten a.m."

"Please have a seat. She's temporarily detained."

Chafing, Harry didn't like to be kept waiting. He glanced at his watch pointedly—not that it was the young lady's fault. He motioned at the leather sofa a few feet away. "We'll be right over here."

A few moments later, a short fifty-year-old Haitian woman in a hotel uniform joined them.

"*Bonjour*. I am Chantale Veilleux, the assistant manager. I'm afraid Ms Thompson was called away on an emergency. She'll be with us as soon as she can. Would you like to join me? I'll get you set up in your office."

"Thank you. I'd appreciate that." He showed a mouthful of teeth, glad that he'd had braces as a kid. Rising to his feet, he let her lead the way. His team members brought up the rear.

When they reached the office beside Deanna Thompson's, Chantale stopped in front of it. "This will be your headquarters during your stay. Please make yourself at home and start setting up. Can I get you coffee, water, or soda? If you're hungry, we have a full service restaurant and a gift shop with many snacks. I'd be happy to show you where they are."

"Coffee would be nice. I take it with one cream only." He hadn't had his caffeine rush yet today and needed something to kick-start him.

His assistants both requested bottled water.

While they waited, they got out their equipment, including the K2 meters and thermal imaging readers.

As minutes turned into an hour and his stomach growled, Harry began to grow irked. He wondered what the emergency was and why it was taking so long.

A large flash of red outside the window caught his attention and he looked closer, past the palm trees and saw grass. It was a fire engine and an ambulance. Several firemen and a couple of EMTs alighted from their vehicles and entered the hotel. He wondered if they had anything to do with the emergency Deanna was dealing with. Since no fire alarms were going off, he assumed that there wasn't a fire. It must be a medical emergency.

Deciding to take up the assistant manager on her offer of lunch, he headed out of the door. As he reached the doorway, he bumped into Deanna. He shot his hands out to hold her steady and he muttered, "Sorry, I didn't see you. Are you okay?"

She laughed lightly, seductively. "I'm fine. I didn't see you either."

He backed up to allow her entry as he took inventory of her. Despite an absence of makeup — except for mascara — her skin glowed and her lips were plump and kissable. Her hair bounced in a long ponytail, lush and curly. The hotel uniform accentuated her curves, making her look luscious. Then he tried to back away from his thoughts, unwilling to feel that way about a client, especially one who disdained his line of work. "We were just about to get a bite of lunch at your hotel restaurant. Would you be available to join us?"

"I'd love to. My treat." She put her hand on the jamb. "I'm sorry I'm delinquent. A guest had to be cut out of the bathtub. She got her toe stuck in the faucet and she was having a panic attack that triggered an asthma attack."

"We wondered what the fire truck and ambulance were here for."

When she spun on her heel and sashayed away from the offices, he followed. He had trouble keeping his gaze off her well-rounded ass.

When they reached the restaurant, they gathered at a table for four. His legs brushed the white tablecloth that hung halfway down to the floor and spread across his lap. He positioned himself across from the manager to have the best view of her, letting Bruno and his other assistant, Keri, sit beside her.

Before they started discussing business matters, they studied the menu. Upscale dishes populated the bill of fare, including Steak Diane, blackened tilapia and lobster risotto. He took a sip of the iced water in front of him and leaned back in his chair, eyeing the delicious-looking food.

Soon a redheaded young waiter, who looked to be barely college age and was dressed in an elegant white uniform, appeared at Deanna's side, his pen poised over his order pad. "Are you ready to order?"

The manager's face glowed with a dawning smile so that Harry had to wrench his gaze away from her. Carefully, he fixed it on the waiter. After Deanna ordered a Lagniappe salad with a raspberry iced tea, he ordered the blackened tilapia.

Before the others could order, Deanna scowled and leaned forward. "I'm sorry, but that's not on the menu at the moment. Order anything else you want."

Disappointed, he looked over the menu and selected an alternate dish. "How about the Hibachi Steak with shitake mushrooms and red wine?" He winked at Deanna. "Don't worry. I'll pick up the tab."

"Excellent choice, sir." The young man jotted down his order.

"You don't have to." Deanna blushed charmingly and looked away. Her long, dark lashes swept down, veiling her soulful eyes.

"I insist. There are three of us. One of you." In good conscience, he couldn't order such an expensive menu item on someone else's tab. Especially not such an attractive woman's.

"Thank you."

"You're welcome. You can treat me next time."

Color rose higher in her cheeks and she bit her lip.

Man, but he wanted to pull that lip into his mouth with his teeth and taste it. She might not know it but she was adorable.

Finally, Bruno and Keri ordered and the waiter left them.

"Is there a story about the fish?" He quirked an eyebrow, his sixth sense kicking in.

Groaning, Deanna looked sheepish. She reached around and massaged the back of her neck. "This morning seven guests claimed they were so ill they had to go to the emergency room. All ate our blackened tilapia last night. We're investigating the cause now."

"Ouch," he commiserated with her.

"Worse, someone called the press so it will probably be in the papers by this evening, maybe even on TV. Hotel management has its share of challenges." A wistful smile played around her lips.

"I'm sure it does. Ghosts top your list, I imagine."

She stared him down, her gaze narrowing. "*If* the perpetrators of these shenanigans are poltergeists. You know, my head chef even tried to blame the tainted fish on them."

He doubted the spirits had poisoned the fish, but he didn't want to give her fuel to disbelieve in spirits, so he kept mum. Highly annoyed, he challenged, "After witnessing those bowling pins flying at you, you still disbelieve?"

She folded her arms on the table and leaned toward him, fixing him with a steady stare as though Bruno and Keri weren't there. "There has to be a reasonable explanation. Maybe someone replaced the pins with lightweight floatables or remote-control ones."

"Why? For what purpose? Did you find out if your owners have any enemies?"

"No. Not that I've been able to discern."

"Then that's highly unlikely." *Floatable bowling pins? Flying remote-control bowling pins?* He'd never heard such tripe.

"As unlikely as real live apparitions? I know you make your living looking for ghosts, but do you honestly find them?"

"Whoa!" He stood so fast his chair clattered to the floor with a loud clang. Suddenly she didn't seem so delectable. All he wanted to do was throttle her and shake some sense into her. "Are you accusing us of being scam artists?"

"Boss," Bruno said in a low, warning voice. "You have an audience."

Well aware that their fellow patrons had twisted in their seats to watch the show, he picked up the chair and sat again. Seething, he tried to calm himself. But it wasn't easy. He started to rake his hands through his hair and stopped himself. He wouldn't give her the satisfaction of looking nervous.

"Do you *really* want us here? Why did you bother to call us?"

When she opened her mouth, he interrupted, still furious. "I'll tell you why you called us—you want us to disprove the hauntings theory. Maybe you need the cops if you're that sure you have human monsters instead of ghosts."

"Ghosts?" patrons at nearby tables repeated, their eyes widening.

"Way to go. Broadcast it to our entire clientele," she said in a harsh whisper.

"The entire city knows your hotel is haunted." 'Duh' hung in his voice. "Maybe you should embrace it and play it up to ghost hunters and the like."

"Most of our clientele is from out of town. And just how many spirit hunters are there to keep us afloat? We have fifteen hundred units to rent nightly."

"I don't think we're the right company for your needs." He dug his credit card out of his pocket and called for the waiter to come over. When the young man joined them, he handed the card over. "Here, charge our food and pack it up. We have to go."

"Please don't," Deanna said, biting her lower lip. "I— We need you. I'm sorry if I insulted you and I promise to watch my tongue. I also will do my best to keep an open mind. Those bowling pins flying about in the air were quite unusual and I can't explain it."

Harry kept hold of his card. When she'd said 'I need you', his stomach had clenched. Something deep and primal wanted her to need him. Then he berated himself and a growl rose from deep in his throat.

Finally, he said, "Fine. We'll stay on the condition that you have to work with us. You will respect us. You will provide us with whatever we need, including access to any part of the hotel we deem fit. *Capisce*?"

Nodding, she thrust out her hand to shake. "Understood on all counts."

He shook her hand and was unprepared for the electricity that zinged between them. When she jerked her hand back, he wasn't surprised. He wasn't sure what to think about all this either.

The food came moments later, smelling heavenly. He sniffed appreciatively before taking a bite. "Yum! This is awesome. I'd like to meet the chef."

He recalled the man with horns rushing out of the hotel in a chef's uniform. "He isn't the dude with the devil horns, is he?"

"Bingo. His name's José. We have some rather, uh, colorful employees. In fact, I have some interviews lined up for later today. We're rather short-staffed so I'm afraid I'll have to leave you to your own devices after our lunch is over."

"We'll need to meet José to question him about the strange happenings in the kitchen. Didn't you say that gourmet dishes appear out of nowhere overnight, often prepared from food not in stock? And that sometimes knives fly around the kitchen?" Harry made notes on his iPad, clicking away with his stylus.

"Yes. We'll schedule an appointment for you to interview him between the lunch and dinner rushes."

"We'd also like to set up our monitoring equipment overnight in the kitchen. We might as well start tonight. Has anything happened in the kitchen since you've been here?"

"Not to my knowledge. Only in the bowling alley." Deanna forked some lettuce and tomato and lifted it to her mouth. Then she chewed delicately. After that, she washed it down with a sip of tea.

A half hour later after, they'd completed their meal and paid for it. Deanna escorted them to the kitchen, introduced them to José and his crew then set up a meeting time that was mutually agreeable.

Afterward, she took them to the security office. "I'd like you to meet our director of security, Emily Spencer. I'll leave you in her capable care so you can pick her brain. I'm off to conduct interviews."

* * * *

The human resources director and recruiter had both walked with the ex-manager so Deanna was stuck doing all the interviewing for new staff. First on the docket was hiring new HR employees. At least the payroll person was still on staff so everybody was being paid.

Her first appointment was with Claudette Myles, a forty-seven-year-old Chinese Jamaican woman who had applied for the position of recruiter. She was a slight woman with straight, shoulder-length, black hair and sloe-dark eyes. Her professional suit matched her well-polished high heels and leather purse.

When she shook Deanna's hand, however, her weak grip reminded her of a limp fish. "It's nice to meet you. Please join me in my office and have a seat across from me."

Claudette smoothed her skirt beneath her as she sat demurely and curled her legs under her chair. Then she set her purse on the floor beside her.

Quickly re-reading Claudette's resume, Deanna tried to keep her expression neutral. It looked promising. The candidate had a lot of notable experience, not only in personnel but also in hotels. "Please tell me about yourself."

"Well, you'll be very happy if you hire me. I am the best in the business. I have very low attrition rate in my hires."

"That's good as we've had a very high attrition rate. It seems our hotel has a reputation for being haunted."

Claudette's eyes grew large with terror. "As in ghosts? Real ghosts?"

"I don't personally believe in ghosts. We're in the process of checking out the reports and solving the problem."

The woman started screaming in an indiscernible Jamaican patois and grabbed her bag. The only words Deanna understood were 'ghosts' and 'spirits' as she ran past her in a flurry.

Wiggling her fingers after the interviewee Deanna sighed and murmured, "Bye-bye."

She had a few minutes until her next interview so she read over the applications. Many were extremely underwhelming and it seemed that she had slim pickings. Her next appointment with an Ethan Newman sounded promising, however. Like the woman before him, he had a lot of experience.

When Mr Newman arrived, she greeted him warmly. A silver tie clasp and cufflinks accentuated his pinstriped suit and bright blue tie. She could see her reflection in his highly polished shoes.

"Welcome, Mr Newman. I'm pleased to meet you. I'm Deanna Thompson, general manager of The Gilroy. I'll be interviewing you today."

He offered her a firm, strong handshake that she liked. She motioned for him to take the chair across from her and she was impressed that he waited for her to sit first before he folded his length into his seat.

"Please tell me about yourself."

"I was the human resources director at my last two companies, which spanned the past thirteen years. Unfortunately, however, I've been unemployed since last year, because of the bomb threat in my prior company. They accused me—unfairly mind you. The police couldn't prove anything."

"I'm sure." Her nerves jumped and she tried not to fidget. Yet it felt like ice had frozen her veins.

"Employers shouldn't piss off their workers. It's very unwise, you know. It was all their fault!"

"It sounds like it." Her temples began to throb and she'd give anything for a couple of tablets of pain reliever. She was so glad she wasn't a full-time recruiter. Did they run into nutcases like this all the time?

"Don't worry. My counselor says it will probably never happen again. He thinks that I'm most likely cured. When do I start?"

Swallowing hard, Deanna tried to gauge her words carefully. She didn't want to infuriate him and wind up with an ax in her back. "We're still in the interviewing process. We'll be in touch if we select you for a second interview."

Ethan jumped up and pointed a shaky finger at her. "Oh sure! Give me the royal kiss-off. You hear 'bomb threat' and you immediately become judgmental. You'll be sorry! Just wait and see."

"I'm sorry but I must insist you leave now." She didn't accept threats and she picked up her phone and started dialing Emily Spencer. "I'm calling our security."

"I'm going." On his way out, he banged his fist on her desk then he slammed her door with gusto.

"Emily Spencer here."

"It's Deanna. Please make sure the tall swearing man in the blue pinstripe suit leaves the premises without incident. He threatened me."

"Do you want to press charges with the police?"

She gazed out of the window at the cloudless blue day through the palm tree fronds that swayed lazily in the soft Miami breeze. "It was a veiled warning. He didn't come right out and threaten. But he made a bomb threat to his last company and he's one big toe short of a foot."

"Yes, boss. I'll escort him off the property."

"Be careful. He's a real piece of work." She was beginning to see why they had such a strange cast of characters at this hotel.

Next, a thirty-two-year-old woman by the name of Madison Perry waltzed in with long black hair streaked in bright red highlights, obviously fake eyelashes, caked on foundation and bright red lipstick. She wore boot-cut blue jeans, boots, a red leather jacket and she carried an oversized purse. She also chewed a large wad of gum.

"How ya doin'? What does this gig pay?"

Blinking, Deanna couldn't believe that someone would apply for a human resources job in such attire or speak so casually.

"I'm doing well, thank you. How are you?" She led the way to her office and motioned for the younger woman to sit in her guest chair.

When Madison plopped into her chair, she let her purse fall to the floor. It opened so that Deanna could see a large hotel vase inside.

Nonplussed, she couldn't believe her eyes. Then she excused herself and told the applicant she'd be right back. She stepped next door and called Emily Spencer. She requested to have a security guard come and apprehend the thief.

Madison protested that she didn't steal the vase, that it was hers. When they showed her the hotel's engraved name on the bottom of the vase, she changed her story and insisted that someone was framing her and had slipped the vase unnoticed into her purse.

Fed up with the woman's lies, Deanna told Emily Spencer to call the police and file a complaint. "I'm not going to put up with theft in our hotel. I can't believe she had the nerve to steal it then bring it into my office right under my nose. She must think I'm an idiot."

"Obviously you're not," Emily Spencer said commiseratively. "You caught her immediately."

"We're no closer to finding our human resources staff than we were before I started."

"What's going on outside?" Emily pointed out of the window and squinted.

Following the head of security's line of vision, she spied an older woman in just a bra standing by her open car door. As she watched, the person shrugged into a suit jacket and buttoned it. Then she pulled off her jeans and stood in just her underwear before pulling up a skirt. "Is that woman really dressing in our parking lot?"

"That's what it looks like." Emily shook her head. "It takes all types."

Beginning to think that Emily was the only other sane person in the hotel, Deanna couldn't stop watching the train wreck outside. She wondered why the woman hadn't come inside to change in her room or, if not a guest, in a restroom.

When the same woman presented herself as the next contender, Deanna almost laughed aloud in her face. She was out of the running before saying a word about wasting her time. Still, Deanna shook her hand and greeted her cordially. She wasn't going to call her out on her bizarre behavior. "I'm the general manager,

Deanna Thompson, and I'll be interviewing you today."

"I'm Gloria Vail and I'm pleased to make your acquaintance. Thank you for seeing me."

"Before we get started, I only feel it fair to tell you that this is a haunted hotel. We have quite pesky ghosts."

The woman's eyes lit up with interest. "Really? Ghost hunting is one of my favorite hobbies. Tell me about them."

Pity. She might have fit in here if not for her proclivity for undressing in front of the guests. Deanna gave her a little history but didn't spend too much time, as this wasn't going anywhere.

"I'd love to work here. I do so hope you'll seriously consider me." Gloria stood and smiled hopefully. "When do you expect to make a decision about this position?"

"We still have several interviews." Deanna rose from her seat and took the four steps to the door where she waited for Gloria to join her.

"Oh. I see." Sniffing back tears, Gloria pulled an old tattered tissue from her pocket and dabbed at her eyes. "I really need this job."

Deanna felt sorry for her, but not sorry enough to hire her under the circumstances. Even if she was in the running, she wasn't going to make a snap decision. "I understand. It was a pleasure meeting you, Gloria."

"The pleasure was all mine." Gloria lifted her chin, straightened her shoulders then took her departure.

Chantale popped in. "How is the search going? Did you find any plausible candidates?"

Groaning, Deanna held her head in her hands. "Not even close. I don't know how much longer I can do this. I have two more people to meet with today and some more tomorrow."

"Hang in there. The right people will come along." Chantale hugged her and patted her back.

To think she had thought about putting a directive into place to make everybody wear normal hairstyles, hair color, limit jewelry usage and cover tattoos. At the rate she was going, they'd all mutiny and she'd have no employees left.

As Chantale left, she gave the thumbs up sign.

With a weak smile, Deanna returned the motion.

By five p.m. she was no closer to finding either a recruiter or a director of human resources. The sane people wanted nothing to do with a possibly haunted hotel, or maybe they thought she sounded insane and they desired to steer clear of her. She didn't want anything to do with the crazy people. What an impasse.

Maybe she could find someone just slightly mad, who had a lot of skill and experience. Hopefully the next day would prove better.

A shadow slid across the floor a moment before a rap sounded on the door. "Hey there. Do you have a few minutes to spare?"

Harry's deeply sensual voice wrapped warmly around her, pulling her out of her reverie. Without awaiting invitation, he swaggered in and sank into the seat across from her.

"Please come on in," she said sarcastically. Leaning back in her chair, swiveling from side to side, she regarded him with eagerness. She tried to veil her reaction to him and deliberately remembered what an exasperating man he was and that he believed in ghosts. That did it. She practically scowled.

"I interviewed your kitchen staff. I hope you don't mind, but I also interviewed your bowling alley employees and the housekeeping crew. There are some pretty grave things going on in your hotel. With your permission, I'd like to install more video cameras and our special monitoring equipment in the galley, bowling lanes and the hotel rooms in question."

Tapping her fingers on the desk, she wasn't sure about the hotel rooms. "We'll have to wait until the hotel rooms are unoccupied. There's been a lot of bad press lately about surveillance in hotel rooms. Then we'll set you up in there. We can't book the rooms with surveillance devices." She shivered just thinking about it.

"Well, leave them open for me soon as you can. Unless you want to prolong our stay—and our fees."

Of course, she didn't like the sound of higher charges. Despite herself, however, she liked the idea of extending his stay. What in the hell was wrong with her? She was acting as though she'd never seen an attractive man before. "Excuse me for a moment while I find out."

She checked with her evening concierge, Tabitha. The woman was in her twenties, thin, with spiked red hair and tight little braids that cascaded down the back of her neck. "What is the status of rooms three-fourteen and three-sixteen?"

Tabitha rapidly clicked on the computer keys then peered at the monitor. "Three-fourteen is booked and three-sixteen is vacant."

"I'll take a key to three-sixteen. How long is three-fourteen going to be occupied?" Impatient, she tapped her fingers on the desk.

"It's due to be vacated tomorrow at regular checkout time."

Favoring the woman with a smile, she took the key and instructed, "Book the room for me."

Pleased with her employee's performance, she dug in her pocket and pulled out a lottery scratch-off ticket where the winner could possibly earn a thousand dollars a week. She handed it to her. Deanna enjoyed rewarding her staffers for a job well done. "For you for doing a good job."

Tabitha's hazel eyes lit up and she grinned as she palmed a coin and started scratching it. "Wow! Ten dollars! Thanks!"

"You deserve it." She wondered what would happen if one day one of the tickets was a grand prizewinner. It would probably be bye-bye worker. She'd picked up this practice from a past boss. She didn't think her present employer would mind this out-of-the-box thinking.

Momentarily, she rejoined Harry and his team. "Room three-sixteen is open so you can set up shop in there tonight. You'll have to wait for three-fourteen until tomorrow."

"We'll need to stay for a minimum of a few nights, maybe more, since the ghostly activity usually occurs after dark."

"Okay. Understood." She hoped the owners were ready to throw serious money at this project since they were so insistent on solving the problem.

"Do you need any other assistance from me?" Conversely, she hoped not as she was exhausted from working double and triple shifts all week, yet she had an insane desire to stay close to him.

"Just leave me a phone number to reach you. We should be fine. It might be better if a non-believer isn't around to annoy the ghosts." He fixed her with a wide, sardonic smile.

Damn, but it was almost charming, just like the rest of the man. *Almost...*

He was still infuriating as hell. Maybe after a good night's sleep she'd be better able to deal with him. Besides, she had round two of the applicants from hell to deal with tomorrow so she needed a fresh mind.

* * * *

Luckily, she slept through the night. No one called to interrupt her REM cycles and she felt refreshed the next morning and ready to hold her own with Harry DeVeaux and rein in the craziness of the city-size resort.

This morning, she had time to apply her full makeup, including foundation and lip-gloss. She blow-dried and curled her complete head of hair, not merely half. Then she rolled up her panty hose, slipped on high heels and pinned on her name tag. Ready to meet the challenges of the day, she squared her shoulders, lifted her chin and stepped outside her apartment on the top floor of the main building.

Moments later, she entered the elevator and made her way downstairs. Soon she was grazing at the breakfast buffet. She picked up her favorite fruit, oatmeal and glass of orange juice. Then she bumped into Harry—literally. "Uh, sorry. It's crowded in here."

"You have a decent buffet." He took a bite out of a crisp piece of bacon then put it back on his plate that he'd loaded with French toast, eggs, bacon and sausage. There wasn't a piece of fruit in sight.

She wondered how he kept his manly figure eating so many calories. Then again, men could handle a lot more food than women could without gaining weight. It wasn't fair.

"Care to join me? I have a few things to share with you about last night."

Glancing at her watch, she nodded. "I can spare a few minutes. Our morning managers' meeting doesn't start until nine."

He led her to a table for two in the corner and waited for her to sit before he did. When she unloaded her tray, he took hers and disposed of it. About six foot two, he had to push his chair back several inches to fit at the table. After that, he poured a generous amount of syrup onto his toast before cutting it with the edge of his fork.

"What do you have to tell me?" She picked up a strawberry and bit into it. Then she licked the juice from her lips.

"We picked up paranormal readings on our K2 and thermal imaging analysis monitors. I think you definitely have spirits. Without talking to them, I don't know if they're your Lynette and Grant, though."

"English, please." He was talking gibber jabber and gobbledygook.

He chewed a large piece of French toast before answering. Finally, he said, "It means, we can see images of the ghosts and there are strong electronic-type emissions coming from the room that only appear when apparitions are present."

Digesting that bit of information, she spooned a bite of oatmeal into her mouth. After she swallowed it, she tried to ingest his explanation as well. "Did you just stake out room three-sixteen or did you also check into the kitchen and the bowling alley?"

"We started with three-sixteen. We'll look at three-fourteen tonight then branch out to the kitchen and bowling alley. With your permission, I can bring in more crew members. It'll speed up the process. We can split up."

Since lost room rentals cost money, she made an executive decision. "Please bring more of your team members so you can hurry the progression. We need to fix this problem ASAP."

Her cell phone rang and she pulled it out and squinted at it. The concierge desk was paging her. "Excuse me," she said to him, then cupped her hand around the phone. "Deanna here. How may I be of assistance?"

"This is Teena. Mrs Roxanne Cambridge-Anderson is on the line demanding to speak to you. She's very insistent and not being very nice."

Surprised, Deanna mouthed to Harry, "It's Roxanne Cambridge-Anderson."

Harry's eyes also widened with astonishment. He mouthed back, "What does she want? Does she know what we're doing?"

Not that she was aware of. She hadn't been in contact with her or anyone that would tip her off.

When the call clicked over to the caller, Deanna answered cautiously, "This is Deanna Thompson. How may I help you?"

"I demand to know what you think you're doing, poking around my stepsister's death. You're upsetting her mother, who is quite elderly and in a nursing home. The police made their findings and deemed it a double suicide. I'm warning you to leave it alone," Roxanne said in a stern, possibly threatening tone of voice.

Whoa! "You're *warning me*? Who told her mother? You? It's not common knowledge that we're looking into this." Adrenaline raced through Deanna. "We're just trying to stop the strange goings-on in our hotel. We never said it had anything to do with your stepsister or her fiancé. That's only one theory and a far-fetched one at that."

"If you know what's good for you, Ms Thompson, you will not cross me. Drop your line of investigation this instant," Roxanne said in very imperious, clipped tones.

Ice slushed through Deanna's veins and she tried to quell the fear that threatened to run rampant through her. She might not believe in ghosts, but she very much believed in the wrath and power of mighty socialites with too much clout, especially one who was a possible murderess.

A scowl grew larger on Harry's face the longer the conversation lasted. He leaned forward as though he wanted to listen in and perhaps catch the other side of the discussion.

"Hang up. Don't talk to her anymore." Harry tried to grab the phone from her.

Deanna ducked out of his reach and said to her aggressor, "This conversation is finished. Good day."

Shaken, she turned back to Harry. "Do you think we should involve the police? Maybe she did murder her stepsister and the fiancé. Perhaps she is behind our troubles."

"Let me do more digging first. Typically, the cops don't take well to paranormal investigations. They tend to disregard it as soothsaying." He shoveled in a mouthful of scrambled eggs then pushed his food around his plate.

"Okay. Unless she shows up or calls again. Then no promises." She couldn't abide people who threw their weight around. And threats really sent her reeling.

No longer hungry, she looked at her watch and stood. "I have to go to my meeting. Let me know if you need anything. Emily Spencer is a good resource too."

Standing, he saluted sharply and tapped his heels together. "Aye-aye, *el capitan*."

* * * *

Before she reached the morning meeting, Deanna was waylaid by an expectant mother, crying and moaning in the lobby. The young woman, who was heavily pregnant and with an otherwise very slim frame, grabbed her arm. "Please help me. Call nine-one-one. I don't think I can make it to the hospital. Something's very wrong."

The floor felt slick beneath her feet. Deanna looked down. She was standing in a puddle of water, or was it amniotic fluid? "Did your water just break?"

Nodding, the young woman winced. "It just gushed out. I'm only seven months pregnant and I'm having twins. This is too early."

Oh, my God. Oh, my God.

About to hyperventilate, as delivering babies wasn't in her job description, she dragged her phone out of her pocket and dialed nine-one-one. Flustered, she instructed the dispatcher to send emergency straight to The Gilroy's main building's lobby. Then she called out to Brenna and Teena, "Have Emily Spencer and at least two members of her crew and Chantale come here right away. Tell Sydney to bring a lot of towels and hot water. Find the closest empty room on the first floor and let me know what number it is." She wasn't exactly sure what to do with the towels and hot water but all the movies demanded them in all the birthing scenes.

Thumbs hooked in his jeans pockets, Harry ambled over to them. "Do you need some assistance?"

Doubting that he could help in this matter, she arched an eyebrow. "Do you know anything about delivering babies?"

"I was a medic in the Coast Guard. I had to help bring a baby into the world once. First, we need to get the mother to a bed or at least a couch."

She was glad to be proven wrong this time and she gave him a wavering smile. "I'm working on a bed. We don't have one set up yet."

He looked around the lobby. "A couch is better than nothing."

Through gritted teeth she said, "She's having twins. I called nine-one-one and the cavalry."

Emily Spencer and her team arrived a moment later. "Brenna says room one-twelve is ready. We'll move her there. Do you think she can walk with help?"

"I don't think so." Deanna didn't appreciate that they were attracting a crowd and they couldn't allow her to give birth in the middle of the lobby. It wouldn't be a good experience for their other guests either.

"Please have your guards disperse the crowd. The mother doesn't need this on top of everything else." Deep lines etched around Harry's lips. "Perhaps your guards can carry her? We have to be very gentle so as not to hurt the mother or the babies."

She could feel a lawsuit coming on if she made the wrong move. Where in the hell was the city ambulance? They had taken forever to come when the last medical emergency had happened the other day as well. It felt like they were lollygagging again today.

"I can help too," Harry said. "Point me in the direction of one twelve." Harry looked at the young mother. "Tell me your name, darlin'," he drawled.

Panting, the young woman said, breathless, "Scarlet. Scarlet Brighton. I came with my husband on his business trip. I didn't want to stay alone at home."

"Everything's going to be okay. The EMTs are on the way and we're going to be here with you until they arrive." As if he'd done this a hundred times before, Harry's demeanor was calm and soothing. Even Deanna started to breathe easier.

Deanna called out to Brenna and Teena. "Send the EMTs to room one-twelve. We're taking her there." To Sydney she said, "Please have your crew clean up the lobby."

The trip to room one-twelve seemed to take an eternity. Harry picked the woman up and carried her to the room, escorted by one of the guards.

Deanna led the way, opening the door then turning down the bedsheets.

On her heels, Sydney brought in an armful of towels and one of his crew members carried water. He laid out several towels on the bed before Harry laid the soon-to-be mother on the mattress.

Scarlet writhed and screamed. She fisted the sheets in her hands, pulling them off the mattress. "Please. Call. My. Husband. His. Number's. In. My. Phone."

Kneeling on one knee beside her, Harry smoothed tendrils of her errant hair away from her perspiring face. "What's his name, darlin'?"

"Matt. Brighton." A ragged breath punctuated each word. She latched onto Harry's hand, her knuckles paling when she clenched her fist.

When she squeezed his fingers so tightly they turned crimson, his smile thinned into an almost invisible line. "It's okay. Just hold onto me, darlin'. I'll stay with you until Matt can get here."

Impressed by his warm bedside matter, Deanna watched their interaction. She timed the contractions, concerned that they were only one and a half minutes apart.

"Oh. God. I. Have. To. Push."

"Don't push, Scarlet. We're not ready yet." Harry motioned for Deanna to hold Scarlet's hand while he checked Scarlet's cervix.

It felt like Deanna's fingers were being fractured one bone at a time and she realized she was doing the Lamaze breathing with the mother.

When Harry said, "She's crowning. We're going to have a baby now," Deanna held Scarlet's hand with both of hers.

Sydney helped Harry into a pair of sanitized gloves.

"It's going to be okay. He's done this before," Deanna said this as much for her sanity as for the young woman's.

Positioning himself between the mother's legs and holding out his gloved hands to catch the infant, Harry's forehead pinched. "Are those EMTs here yet? Don't they have a GPS?"

Looking up at the Amazon security guard Deanna directed, "Emily, please call and see what the delay is."

"Right away, boss." Emily walked to the corner of the room and turned her back to the group. She bent her head to her phone and murmured something indiscernible.

"It's coming," Harry said in a stage whisper as the mother grunted and pushed.

Then a baby squealed.

Harry cried, "It's a girl! Somebody take it. There's another one trying to come out."

Sydney put a towel over his arms and took the child. He rocked the infant, cooing to it.

Two EMTs sprinted into the room, dragging a stretcher and other equipment. "We'll take over from here."

"You're a bit late," Harry said, holding up the second baby. "It's a boy."

One of the EMTs, a well-built bald man of medium height, patted Harry on the shoulder. "Good job, man. We'll take the tots."

"Where is she? Where are they?" A young man with long hair hanging down to his shoulders ran into the room wearing a wrinkled business suit and a worried expression.

Feeling protective like a mother grizzly bear, or rather like a grandmother grizzly bear, Deanna blocked his way. "Who are you?"

"Scarlet's husband. Matt Brighton." He dug into his pocket and brought out his ID, flashing it.

Relieved that everybody was finally in place, Deanna stepped aside and let him through. She hoped the EMTs would be able to remove them shortly to a safer, more appropriate place. Wondering what time it was, she glanced at her watch. Nine thirty-three a.m. She would have guessed it to be noon. Maybe they could still have a semblance of their morning meeting.

Before long, the EMTs moved the young couple and their offspring to the ambulance and took them to the hospital. She left the clean-up in Sydney's capable hands. Not only did she hand him a couple of scratch-off tickets, but she also murmured to him privately, "You should apply for the head of housekeeping position. I'll give you a good reference with the boss."

"Yes, boss." Sydney smiled and bowed. "I'd be honored."

"You did an excellent job today. Let's hope we don't have a repeat of this stressful day." Hot and sweaty, she needed a shower. She looked around for Harry, disappointed that he was gone. The man was as ephemeral as the specters he was chasing.

"No, ma'am. Let's hope not. Once was more than enough. However, we'll know what to do if we have to deliver more babies." The older man backed away and began gathering the soiled linens. He called for back-up. Within moments, his crew showed up to help.

Wiped out, Deanna needed a cup of caffeine to get pumped up again. She made a beeline to the staff lunchroom and poured coffee into a mug. What she really needed was some espresso, but no one had brewed any today. She'd take what she could get.

Feeling a bit more energized, Deanna rotated her head to work the kinks out of her neck and shoulders. Then she shook out her arms.

"That was something else." Harry's voice washed over her from behind.

Unprepared for him, she threw her hand to her throat and jumped. "Don't sneak up on me like that. What if I'd had hot coffee in my hands? What are you doing in the employees' lounge?"

"A contractor is an employee—of sorts. I need a coffee fix too after that. Man, but that was intense. You did a good job in there." Without invitation, he poured brew into a Styrofoam cup, added a couple of sugars then took a sip.

"Me? You were the star of the show. I don't know what we would have done without you."

"Do I get a scratch-off ticket too, for a job well done?" Harry wiggled his brows.

"Why not? You saved me from being the midwife." She chuckled, dipped in her pocket, and tore off a couple of scratch-offs then handed them to him. "Don't say I never gave you anything."

"Thanks. I won't." He used his fingernail to scratch away. Glancing up at her he asked, "Does your staff really respond to getting these?"

Nodding, she said, "Pretty well. Of course, if someone wins a million bucks off a ticket I bought, I may have to shoot myself."

Harry chuckled. "Yeah, that would suck."

A shadow fell across the floor. Chantale stuck her head through the open doorway. "There you are. Should I gather the managers for our meeting?"

"Please. We'll make it short." She turned to Harry, who was lounging against the counter regarding her with a lazy charm that made her knees go weak. "Excuse me. Duty calls."

"Lunch at noon in your restaurant? Or we can run down the street to that little French bistro so no one can disturb us. I have a few things to go over with you."

Her heart thumped hard against her ribs. "I should be able to. Okay. Yes." Over her shoulder she called, "Gotta run. See you later at the French bistro."

Several times during the meeting, she caught herself glancing at her watch, frowning, wishing it was almost noon. Trying to keep her mind on business, she peered at Natalie, her marketing director. "How are we doing at overbooking rooms? Are we selling out most nights?"

Natalie, a blonde with her hair shaved on one side, long on the other, nodded. "We had to walk two rooms down the street last night. The guests weren't at all happy that we had overbooked and had to find other accommodations for them."

"How are our concierges trained to walk guests? Do they make it seem like we're giving them a reward? It's all in the presentation. Do we offer them a free night at a sister resort, all expenses paid?"

Natalie bent her head over her iPad and click-clacked notes onto it. "I'll make sure we do that."

"We've got to maximize profits. With that said, how are incidentals selling? You know, liquor and snacks in the room. And room service? Restaurant meals? Spa services?"

She listened to the reports and watched over the accountant's shoulder as she added totals to the spreadsheet. Finally, she adjourned the meeting, her mouth dry. She was direly needing a glass of cold water.

Stopping by the closest fountain, she took a sip. Then, eager to meet Harry, she visited her apartment, picked up her purse and got out her keys before heading for her car.

When she neared the car, a bright flash blinded her. Super intense heat scorched her. Her brother's beloved Mustang exploded, throwing her backward. She collided with something hard that knocked her out.

Chapter Four

"Are you okay? What the hell happened?" Harry asked as he cradled her head in his lap. He rocked her gently back and forth, his gaze filled with concern. They were back by the hotel, but she didn't remember being thrown back that far. He must have carried her.

Her head fuzzy, her wobbly thoughts collided. Her bruised, scraped body ached and stung, and the wind had been knocked out of her, but there was no major pain. "I think I'm okay." She let out a cry of dismay. "My car!"

Her pride and joy, a 1970 Mustang rebuilt by her late brother, Dan, once a beautiful metallic blue with a convertible top, sat engulfed in flames. Worse, fire had claimed the cars on either side of it as well.

"Jesus! Maybe somebody *is* out to get The Gilroy. Or is anybody upset with you personally?" he questioned.

"Remember Roxanne Cambridge-Anderson threatened me this morning? She's the only one."

Emily Spencer ran outside, followed by three of her crew members. The guards moved the growing crowd back to a safe distance. They wouldn't allow people to move cars that were parked too close to the fire for fear they might get caught in another explosion. Angry voices rose, some threatening to sue the hotel.

"Oh my God! Are you okay, boss? I called nine-one-one," Emily said, sounding breathless. "Emergency services are on the way."

A moment later, sirens blasted in the air and a parade of trucks, ambulances and police vehicles sped into the lot. Immediately firefighters jumped out of the trucks, hooked up fire hoses and started dousing the blazes. A policeman approached a security guard, who pointed them in Emily's direction.

"You should go to the hospital and get checked out," Emily said to Deanna.

Waving off the ridiculous suggestion, Deanna said with a scowl, "No. I'm required to be here. And I need to call my car insurance company."

"We'll handle everything here and you can take care of matters with your car after you're fixed up." Straightening her bony shoulders, the older woman fixed her stern gaze on Deanna.

"Really, I'm fine." Deanna tried to stand, but suddenly woozy, she swayed and returned to the safety of Harry's arms.

"Emily's right. You should go and get checked out. You could have a concussion or whiplash. I saw what happened and you were thrown pretty hard. You still seem dizzy." Harry kept her in the circle of his arms, steadying her.

God, but Harry's arms were secure and warm and oh so good. She'd be fine if she could stay right where she was for a couple of hours. "But I have interviews to conduct this afternoon."

"They can be rescheduled. You're more important." Emily beckoned the EMTs and pointed at Deanna. "Take her to the hospital. She was thrown in the blast. She should be checked out."

A swarthy, middle-aged, bearded man nodded and called his partners. "Bring a gurney."

Within moments, they'd helped Deanna onto a stretcher.

Before they loaded her into the ambulance, two police officers interrogated her. When Harry told them that Roxanne Cambridge-Anderson had threatened her that morning, they pooh-poohed it. He exchanged a look with Deanna that clearly said he thought the cops were still in the powerful woman's pocket.

She didn't doubt it.

Although the EMTs tried to lift her gently into the ambulance, they set her down bumpily and she let out a moan. Hitting concrete, probably skidding across it several feet, didn't do a body good. What a way to get a good case of road rash!

They injected her with something.

As the medics closed the back doors, Harry called out, "I'll meet you at the hospital. You shouldn't be alone."

She started to nod but a sharp pain riddled her head so she tried to keep still. Unfortunately, the road was rutted with potholes and speed bumps.

What felt like an hour later, they finally wheeled her into the emergency room. Somehow, Harry had bullshitted his way into joining her and he held her hand and talked about this and that to keep her mind occupied until a nurse collected her.

An orderly wheeled her to the x-ray department first. Then she had a CAT scan. After that, she was given more immunizations and her knees, elbows, and forehead bandaged where she had large scrapes. Finally, what seemed backward to her, she took care of her medical insurance and was released.

"Whoa! It looks like you were in a war." Harry looked her up and down and, with commiseration, pushed her to the hospital's lobby in a wheelchair.

She offered him a crooked smile and gingerly touched her forehead. "I must look like a fright. My head's pounding a mile a minute too."

"I'll take you home. But you should rest. Let Chantale and Emily take care of everything. Same goes for tomorrow, if you feel the least bit bad."

"Who died and made you my boss?" She cocked her head and gave him an innocently sweet smile.

"Doctor's orders. I'm just the messenger." He looked at the nurse. "I'll get the car and bring it around."

His car was a gold Grand Jeep Cherokee. He parked at the curb, hopped out then ran around to open the door and help her in. Then he fastened the seatbelt around her.

"I thought your type was dead and buried with the dinosaurs."

"You don't like gentlemen?" He quirked an eyebrow and wrinkled his nose.

"Very much. I just haven't met one in ages. In my line of work men usually yell, swear, cuss and threaten." Too many bad memories plagued her of unhappy, bitchy men. There was no pleasing all the people all the time no matter how hard one tried. Sometimes she thought about changing careers. Today was one of those days. This was the first time someone had tried to kill her. Or was it a coincidence?

It sure didn't feel like a coincidence.

Dan's poor car! It had been all she had to remember him by, except for a couple of pictures. He'd adored that car, spent hundreds of hours refurbishing it and many more driving it around. He'd entrusted his baby to her and now it was toast.

"What time is it?" She'd lost all track of time, although the sun was still up.

"Six. Are you hungry?"

"No. But if you are, please get yourself something. Don't let me stop you." Food was the last thing on her mind. In fact, her stomach roiled now that a meal had been mentioned.

"You have to eat something. At least a bowl of soup. I insist."

"Has anybody ever told you how pushy you are?"

He cracked a grin and drawled, "A few. You need to get something in your stomach. You missed lunch *and* dinner. You'll pass out."

His line of reasoning sounded logical, but her stomach really didn't agree. "Just chicken soup."

"Does your restaurant serve it? Although I'd rather not stop there. If we eat in the dining room at your hotel, you'll be swamped with well-wishers and curiosity seekers. You need your rest. We'll stop somewhere near here, away from the hotel."

"Okay." She wasn't up to a lot of questions tonight. The only person she wanted to talk to besides Harry was the insurance adjustor. And perhaps a private investigator.

He swung the car into a parking lot of a deli that stayed open for dinner, a rarity in Miami. Most only opened for breakfast and lunch.

She let herself hold his hand for steadiness and tried to ignore the electricity that zinged between them and the resulting leap of her heart. Right here in this restaurant were at least two men who were as handsome as Harry, so why did they do nothing for her? It seemed she only had eyes for Harry. So why didn't she like it?

Maybe because he believed in bizarre, creepy shit? And that made him weird. It wasn't that she'd pictured herself with a captain of industry or a larger-than-life romantic hero or a multi-billionaire sheik, but she had pictured herself with a nice, *normal* man she could raise a kid or two with. Not a guy who never grew up and who wanted to be in a *Scooby Doo* cartoon forever. Shaggy was a nice guy too, but he was forever immature.

"Penny for 'em." Harry touched her forearm, above the bandage.

"Huh? What?" She almost reeled on him, feeling guilty for her thoughts, hoping she wasn't transparent.

"What are you thinking so hard about? Steam practically blew out your ears." When a waitress led them to a table, he bowed for her to go first then followed.

"N-nothing important. Just debating if I'll get matzo ball soup or chicken noodle."

"Uh-huh. That wasn't a matzo ball soup kind of face." But he didn't press for an answer.

Since she hadn't had matzo ball soup in ages, she opted for that. He had a turkey club with fries and a Dr Pepper.

"What type of sandwich do you like?"

"I told you. I'm not that hungry." She tilted her head and listened to one of her favorite moldy oldies playing low over the sound system.

"Enquiring minds want to know."

Scrunching her nose, she tilted her head at him. "Why? Next you'll want my whole life story."

"It's just a sandwich for Chrissakes. What's the big deal?" When the waitress slid their food onto their table in front of them, he smothered his fries in ketchup and mixed in a little mustard.

"Ew." It looked like a train wreck.

"So? What type?"

"You've got a one-track mind, don't you?"

"I've been told I'm determined. What type?" He plopped a large fry whole into his mouth and chewed, his gaze never leaving her face.

"Oh all right already. Ham and Swiss on rye with mayo, lettuce, tomato and onion. Are you happy now?"

He motioned the waitress back and ordered her favorite sandwich to go when she brought their bill. "For later in case you get hungry. We'll put it in your fridge."

Frickin' unbelievable. "You're a bully."

He ran a finger around the rim of his water glass. "I'm a caregiver. Somebody has to take care of you if you won't."

Tingles sparkled inside her that he wanted to take care of her. She had to wonder why. They barely knew each other.

"I know you may not want to hear this, but you may need protection. I think someone truly intended to kill you today."

"I think so too. I can't help but think Roxanne Cambridge-Anderson is behind this. But you only just started investigating the suspicious activities. You'd think she'd want the ghosts gone if they might snitch on her."

Harry finished off his sandwich with a big bite then wiped the crumbs off his chin. "Maybe she's afraid the ghosts will finally confide in us, that they wouldn't talk to anybody else. I have a reputation for getting to the bottom of paranormal activity."

"So why not kill you instead of me? You're the ghost whisperer." She batted her lashes at him, only half teasing.

"That would make more sense. Although you're the boss. If you're gone, I'd probably be dismissed. At least she thinks so."

"She mustn't know that the orders to hire you came all the way from my bosses." She slurped the last spoonful of her soup, savoring it.

"I suppose not." He raked his hands through his hair and leaned back in his chair, lifting the front legs off the floor.

"What do we do now? I don't want to drop the investigation but I really don't want to wind up dead."

"Dig deeper. Talk to the ghosts."

She blinked and did a double take. "Have you talked to ghosts, like in that show *The Ghost Whisperer*?"

"Yes, darlin', I have."

She still wondered if he was crazy or gifted. "So you have a special gift?"

"You don't have to have a *gift*. You just have to have an open mind. They've talked to my team too. Do you want to try? Do you think you can do it?"

Honestly, she didn't think she believed. She still thought there was a plausible explanation for the flying bowling pins. "I don't think so."

He dropped the chair with a bang and swore under his breath. "You don't believe your own eyes? I don't understand you!" Jumping to his feet, he whipped out his wallet, tossed a few bills on the table and grabbed the bill. Then he marched to the cash register, not looking back to see if she was following.

Remembering the night in the bowling alley and the video she'd taken, she argued with herself. Someone would have to *want* to go to a lot of trouble to make it look like there were ghosts. The only person she could think of who might want to do so was threatening her to stop the investigation.

Slowly, she followed him as she wrestled with her thoughts. After they slid into his Jeep, she turned to him and took a deep breath. "I'll give it a try. When do we start?"

"Normally I'd say the sooner the better but you need to rest tonight. If you're up to it tomorrow, we'll do it then."

She was feeling rather wiped out, limp and wilting fast. "Sounds like a plan."

But when they reached the hotel, several journalists were waiting to interview her. As she exited the vehicle, they rushed her, thrusting out microphones and talking over each other so that she couldn't understand any of them. Harry tried to shield her and move her past the throng. However, the press blocked their way and blasted out several questions at once.

"Who do you think blew up your car?"

"Do you think someone is trying to kill you personally or are they out to ruin the hotel?"

"Are you involved in illegal activities?"

"Does this have anything to do with the tainted fish that sent several of your guests to the hospital yesterday?"

"What type of injuries did you sustain?"

Her head spinning, her body slumping, she couldn't deal with the press. "Please, I'm not up to this tonight. I was just released from the hospital."

"Just give us a statement we can print."

Harry pushed her behind him. "You heard the lady, pal. No statements. Now let us pass."

"Who are you? Her bodyguard? Her boyfriend? Husband?"

Tension flowed from his body to hers, so palpable she had trouble breathing. She curled her fingers around his biceps, trying to calm him, but he shook her off.

"Don't let them get to you," she said. "This is who they are."

Ignoring her, Harry said, "I'm the guy who's going to shut you up." Then he punched the guy square in the nose.

Cameras clicked and lights flashed as blood spurted from the guy's nostrils and he yelped. The reporter fingered his nose, covering his hand in his blood, and looked at it cross-eyed. "I can't believe you did that. You'll be hearing from my attorney and I'm calling the cops."

"Call away. You're illegally detaining us and blocking guests from entering and leaving the hotel. Now let us pass." Harry glared at the rest of the horde until they parted the waters and let them through.

Moments later, they entered Deanna's apartment and she flopped onto her lounger unapologetically. He found her refrigerator and put her sandwich inside. "Can I get anything for you? Tuck you into bed?"

Warmth flooded her at the thought of him putting her to bed and she hoped she wasn't turning crimson. Trying to hide her discomfort, she picked up the TV remote and pointed it at the cable box. She clicked it on. "I'm just going to watch a show or two until I get sleepy enough to lie down. I'll be fine."

"Make sure you get plenty of sleep. If you're not up to working tomorrow, you are allowed to call in sick." Harry leaned down and deposited a kiss on the tip of her nose.

Surprised, she grew tingly all the way down to her toes, her eyes widening. "Says who? You? I just started this job."

Kneeling by her side, he folded her hand in his. Then he gazed deeply into her eyes with a stern but concerned look. "You're too stubborn for your own good. If you get sick, you'll have to take a lot more time off than one day."

When he absently caressed her hand with his thumb, she shivered. His close proximity was making her heart thump so hard she was afraid he'd feel her erratic pulse and guess what his nearness was doing to her. And why had he kissed her? If you could call that a kiss...

Unable to break eye contact, she was so mesmerized she couldn't move when he reached in and feathered her lips with a soft, tentative kiss.

Even though the contact was ever so slight, flames licked her veins and she wanted—*needed*—more. Cupping his stubbly cheek with the palm of her hand, she held him captive against her mouth as she opened her lips, inviting him inside.

He plunged his tongue into her mouth, seeking, tangling with hers. Then he curled his arms around her and molded her against his heart.

On fire now, she wound her fingers through his thick hair. Against his lips, she murmured huskily, "I don't know what's possessing me to do this. I barely know you."

"You're overthinking this." He crushed her to him, making his desire obvious. He cursed and with a red face, set her aside. "You're not up to this. You need to rest."

Protests began to explode from her lips when the phone rang. As she read the display, she groaned. "Damn! It's the owners." *Like I'll get any rest now.*

* * * *

An hour later, when she'd finally got off the phone with the irate owners then her auto insurance company, she was too wide-awake to go to sleep.

Recalling the less than satisfactory conversation with the owners, Deanna moaned and punched her fist into her other hand. They had threatened to fire her for being incompetent, as if she had arranged for her brother's car to be destroyed. Worse, if that wasn't crazy enough, they'd put her on probation!

She surfed through the cable stations but unfortunately nothing of interest was on TV and her mind kept waffling between the troubling conversation with the owners then back to Harry. Of the two, the thought of Harry was the one that made her smile. She hadn't imagined that kiss, had she? Was she fantasizing again?

Afraid she was, hoping she wasn't, she gave her fantasies free reign. It was far better than dwelling on her tenuous job situation. There wasn't anything more she could do to save her career tonight. Indeed, she began to wonder if this was the right profession for her. Being general manager of such a large resort required complete commitment and she wasn't sure she wanted to give up everything else promising life still had to offer. Like Harry…

Pressing her fingers to her mouth in awe, her lips' swollenness attested to the fact that she had indeed been kissed. Antsy, lonely, unable to get her mind off Harry, she padded over to her laptop and sprawled out with it on her bed. After propping herself up on her pillows and turning on her computer, she went to Facebook. A few moments later, after seeing all the animal funnies and friends complaining that she could stomach, she opened her blog. To her surprise, several comments awaited her from 'ooh la la' to 'you're a whore!'

She blinked at the whore comment but reminded herself that no one knew her true identity. She also told herself that the hotel had been full of romance writers who wrote stuff like this all the time and faced the public without flinching. This was a free country. She had the right to compose what she wanted, even if complete strangers called it smut.

Re-reading her first installment, she was amazed at how well she had nailed him without having met the man. Or had she been influenced by supernatural powers?

Get real, Deanna. She still thought there was a reasonable, non-paranormal explanation for all the strange happenings in the hotel.

Once again, she opened a new page and began to type.

We couldn't get enough of each other. Harry swept me off my feet and carried me to his multi-million-dollar beach house. Wanting to be alone with me, he excused his housekeeper and butler for the day.

Then he swaggered to his bar and asked, "What's your poison?"

"Slow gin fizz, please. However, you don't have to get me drunk to have your wicked way with me." I'd more than proven that.

I looked around his stunning place, so pristine it appeared more like a hotel than a home. Two stories high, the living room had an open ceiling to the top. Floor-to-ceiling windows spanned three sides of the room. The fourth side showcased two balconies with palm trees hanging over.

Everything was white and chrome with clean, square lines. A movie-size TV screen filled the solid wall. Andy Warhol paintings bordered both sides of the TV.

Although the house overlooked a private, untamed beach, there was an oval-shaped pool outside on the blue-tiled deck surrounded by plush orange deckchairs.

He poured our drinks and brought mine to me. When our fingers touched, electricity sparked between us. No doubt we shared something special, even though we'd just met. I didn't doubt that Harry could be my soul mate.

Without asking permission, he stretched out on the couch beside me and rested his hand on my thigh. It felt right, so I didn't complain. Instead, I sidled closer, wanting to be one with him again. Although I'd never believed in it before, I was beginning to wonder if there was such a thing as love at first sight.

Then again, I didn't know anything about the guy, what he did for a living, what he liked to do, what he liked to eat, or even his last name. For heaven's sake, if I wasn't careful, I'd wind up in a hotel room tomorrow morning wearing a wedding band not knowing my own last name, just like one of my favorite country singer's songs.

When he started kissing my neck, I moaned and turned my head to give him better access. Then with my last few remaining brain cells, I managed to ask, "What's your name? Tell me about yourself."

That stopped him cold as though I'd sprayed him with iced water. He looked at me as if I was a hydra. What was wrong with wanting to know my lover's name?

"I'm Harold Xavier Young but everybody calls me Harry. I'm CEO of the CO Corporation, originally from Cleveland,

Ohio. I'm on break and using our company's vacation house. It's mine for two weeks and I just arrived. What are you doing for the next two weeks?"

I crossed my fingers and said what I hoped he wanted to hear. "Staying here with you." At least during my off-duty hours. Maybe I could get a last-minute vacation. I had two weeks coming.

"Tell me about yourself, Thomasina."

Tapping her toes, she paused for several moments thinking about the next scene in her story. What would a real romance writer say? Where did she want her real life to go with Harry?

In the best of all worlds, she'd like to explore her burgeoning feelings for Harry. No doubt heat flared between them the way they argued, the way they had just kissed. But they held such diametrically opposed beliefs that she didn't know if she could live and let live when ghosts were his daily life, not just some vague, passing idea.

She repositioned her fingers on the keys and looked into space, fantasizing.

"I'm an interior decorator. This is a very nice space, by the way. Nice clean lines. I'm single – divorced, no kids. I'm originally from New York."

"Who are you really? What makes you tick?"

"Making love on the beach. In front of the whole wide world. I'm a nudist at heart."

She paused, gaping at her words. Was that make-believe or was this really her fantasy? Did she want to make out on a beach? In front of other people?

Tingles shot through her veins straight to her pussy, and she squirmed. Hell yeah. If she wasn't afraid of getting caught and fired, she'd love to find a swingers club and have an orgy with everybody watching her.

"I'd also like to visit one of those clubs, where they have giant orgies. Where everyone watches everybody else."

Harry kissed the sensitive spot behind my ear, then laved it with his tongue, making me moan and writhe. He caressed my breast, elongating my nipple between his fingers.

Totally on fire, I was about to go up in flames like a volcano. Awesome sensations rippled through me, making my toes curl.

"Let's find one of those clubs."

Surprise and lust raced through me as I raised my head and looked him square in the eyes. "Today?"

"Right now. It's Miami. I bet those places are open twenty-four hours. Give me a sec and I'll check the web." Before I could protest, he lifted me off him then hopped to his feet. He sprinted up the stairs and true to his word was back in a jiffy, a huge grin splitting his handsome face.

"I found a place nearby. We can be there in fifteen minutes. If you really want to go, I'm game."

Excitement made my eyes widen. My pussy thrummed and practically creamed. My nipples beaded. Oh yeah, I was ready. "Yes. I'd really like to go with you now."

"How I love an adventurous, sexy lady." He held out his hand to me with a wicked glint in his eyes. "Let's go."

I couldn't believe I was about to do this or that I had made out with a man I'd just met, especially on a public beach in front of other people. What had happened to me? I was truly wanton and I loved it.

We sat so close together, our thighs rubbing as he sped to the club. He drove with one hand while the other he slid under my shorts and massaged my clit. To return the favor, I insinuated my hand inside his pants and caressed his growing penis.

Groaning, on the brink of coming, I was about to melt into a puddle. "I'm making you feel good, aren't I, baby? Come for me. Clench my fingers." He thrust his fingers into my vagina and rotated them around.

"Oh! Oh! I'm coming." I was so eloquent when I came. I really should have read more Shakespeare and Brontë.

"You're so very wet, so hot, baby. I love it. But you'd better stop touching me before I wreck this car. We're almost there and we can resume then."

Disappointed, but only a little, I nodded and reclaimed my hand. I didn't want us wrapped in metal or having to explain our predicament to a curious policeman.

True to his promise, we pulled into the club parking lot moments later. Vehicles crowded the asphalt from trucks to Jeeps to Lexuses to Pontiacs. A discreet brass nameplate adorned the brick building that merely said — The Club. An imperial canvas awning hung over the entrance. Well-trimmed bushes bordered the perimeter of the structure. Several two-way windows let light shine in while restricting views from the outside.

A ginger-haired doorman in a nice two-piece dark blue suit carded us at the door. Really? I'm thirty-seven and I look at least twenty-seven — twenty-four if I'm having a really good hair day. I found out that Harry was thirty-six but that's okay. I like younger men.

"Please enter and enjoy your visit."

In reality, she had no idea how old the real Harry was. She guessed he was anywhere from thirty-four to forty-five, thus probably older than her. But so what if he was younger? He was darned sexy.

"We will," Harry said with a shit-eating grin. He put his hand in the small of my back and guided me inside.

Suddenly nervous that a client would recognize me, I wondered if I should be here. Would it hurt my business?

Then again, if a client were here, would they care? Still, I really wanted a mask or something to disguise my face. I only wanted my body seen. I leaned close and tiptoed up to Harry. "Do you think they have masks?"

"What? Did you say masks?"

I nodded, trembling.

He said, "I'll find out."

Lo and behold, The Club had half-style face masks galore and didn't seem to think it strange that we wanted them. Harry paid for two, a black one for him that made him look like the Lone Ranger and a very sexy red one with lace for me.

Immediately, I donned my mask. As soon as it was on, I regained my confidence. We did a sensual striptease for each other, then kissed hot and languorously as his cock grew long and thick against my stomach. Eager to feel him inside me again, not willing to wait, I pulled him into the orgy room writhing with gorgeous, naked humanity.

Stunned, even though I had been imagining a sea of nude bodies, big throbbing cocks fucking pussies, fucking asses, and beautiful buxom breasts suckled by ravenous lovers, I stopped dead in my tracks. Not only did I see what I imagined – but more. Threesomes, even foursomes and fivesomes abounded. Lucky women were being fucked by two cocks at once and sometimes also had their mouths full with another penis at the same time.

Harry nudged me. "Is this what you fantasized? Is this what you want?"

Honestly, I hadn't, but now that I was seeing it, I wanted it. "Yes. It looks heavenly," I answered the second question.

He pulled me into his arms and bent me backward, sticking his tongue deep into my mouth. I mated my tongue with his, seeking and learning the cavern of his mouth. I let my hands sift through his soft, dark hair, then I grew bolder and let one hand slide down his flat belly to his curly *mound of hair, to his stiff cock that was obviously ready to make love to me.*

"Fuck me, now, lover," I urged.

"Whatever my baby wants." He swung me into his arms and carried me across the room to a vacant bed large enough for several people. Perhaps he hoped that others would join us. Then he resumed his mind-numbing kisses as he climbed on top of me.

Wanting him so badly an exquisite ache deep inside me, I spread my legs wide and in invitation as he rolled a condom onto his cock. When he thrust into me, I met him and fell into his rhythm. He crushed my breasts against his chest and his heart beat erratically with mine.

Much to my surprise, he whipped us over so that he was on his back and I was on top. I sat up, letting my breasts swing freely as I impaled myself on him. When I felt strange hands on my waist, I jolted for a moment, shocked.

"It's okay, baby. Go with the flow." Harry reached up and caressed my breasts, playing with my nipples, testing the weight of my tits in his palms.

The other set of hands, large with long, sturdy and firm fingers, bit into me gently. Then the person released me and the tip of a latex-covered cock drew up and down over the crack of my ass. Was this really happening to me? Or was I dreaming? If I was dreaming, it was the best darned dream I'd ever had.

But the person worked his cock into my back hole until he began moving in rhythm with Harry and me. The three of us rocked back and forth, and I was filled with two huge, beautiful cocks. I don't know if it was mere moments or an eternity later when my world shattered and I screamed in ecstasy as I came long and hard.

Chapter Five

Just as she had presumed, the owners weren't happy. Not just about the contaminated fish. Not just about exploding cars in the parking lot. Not just about their paranormal investigator punching a reporter in the nose. When she told them about Roxanne Cambridge-Anderson's threat, they were even more displeased than before.

After that, they increased the length of her probationary period, eliciting a string of curses that spilled out under her breath. When her boss asked her to repeat what she'd said, she stumbled on her reply. "I, uh, understand, sir. I'll do better and make you proud."

Although she didn't feel up to par, she reported for work in the morning. She made an extra effort with her hair and makeup so no one would notice that she was under the weather. Instead of wearing high heels, however, she wore flat slippers.

Their daily morning meeting started with enquiries about her health. Then it morphed into questions about who would try to hurt her and who wanted to ruin the hotel's reputation. That made her pause, wondering if she should tell everybody how Roxanne Cambridge-Anderson had threatened her. Could one or more of them be in the woman's pocket? Had one of them planted the bomb in her Mustang?

She hated herself for thinking this way but it couldn't be helped. Right now, she didn't trust anyone. Instead of telling them what she knew and suspected, she asked, "Do you know of anyone who wants to hurt The Gilroy, past or present? Have you seen anything suspicious?"

Chantale piped up. "'Tis said that Lynette Cambridge and her fiancé were murdered by her stepsister, who is now a very powerful woman. I hear she is getting ready to run for state senator. She doesn't want anyone talking to the ghosts."

"But we're trying to rid the hotel of the ghosts — er — whatever is going on here."

As if she was the local expert, Chantale stood and leaned on the table. Her gaze pierced Deanna. "To do that, we have to talk to the ghosts. You may not believe in them, yet you have hired people who do and who are respected in the community too. If she is guilty of murder, it may finally be proven."

Rolling her eyes and raising her hand, Emily Spencer replied, "Even if there were such a thing as ghosts — which I, for one, don't prescribe to — who else would believe that a bunch of apparitions fingered Roxanne for a decades-old murder? Maybe *The Enquirer*."

"There is no statute of limitations on murder. Why is Roxanne threatening me? She must be afraid of something, and I don't think that we're upsetting her mother. Nothing was in the press until the car exploded. Let's hope the reporters don't mention the ghosts. I didn't give them an interview. I hope nobody else here did either." Deanna let her gaze rake over each person in the room. None flinched or looked guilty. Still, there were a lot of other staff members in the hotel who could talk, especially if a reporter waved money under their noses. "I want all of you to have a meeting with your teams and stress the importance that no one speaks to the press or anybody else about private hotel matters. The only people who can speak for The Gilroy are Chantale and myself. We may have to hire a PR person if this keeps up, but I hope not."

That reminded her that she had to resume interviews later in the afternoon. She bit back a groan. She was not cut out to be a recruiter.

"Please remember that everybody signed a confidentiality agreement and the owners will prosecute anybody who violates it. They *strongly* reminded me of this last night. They are not happy about the spoiled fish, the explosions, the threats or the supposed ghosts. We have to solve these mysteries ASAP."

Tapping her fingers on the table, Emily looked like she wanted to say something. Finally, she spoke up. "I think we should hire a private detective to find out who planted the explosive and who's behind all these other strange activities."

"My thoughts exactly. I'll look into it." That reminded her of her car and the others that had caught on fire next to it. She looked at Chantale. "Did you check into our insurance coverage for the cars damaged on our property yesterday? Do we have full coverage?"

"*Oui*, we're up to date. We'll cover the car repairs. I'm working on the paperwork with the car owners now."

Deanna wrinkled her nose. "Repairs? Weren't they burned to a crisp like mine? We'll have to pay bluebook value, perhaps more. God, this is a PR nightmare. I think we really will need a PR person— *and* an attorney. I'll see if the owners have a lawyer on retainer."

"On a more chipper note, the mother and babies are doing well. They send their thanks to all who helped in the delivery." Sydney wore a grin so big it split his face, as though he was the proud papa. "The happy parents are telling everyone what a good job our hotel did."

Glowing from the high praise that her staff well deserved, Deanna said, "That's the kind of stuff the press should be printing. Hopefully they'll leave a nice review on our blog."

"Blog? We have one entry that's about two years old. There's no review section. Our previous manager was afraid of reviews." Chantale shook her head, pursing her lips as the sunlight streaming through the window shimmered off her lip-gloss.

"The more I hear, the more I think we have no choice but to hire a PR person. Everybody has a blog and all hotels have a review section. We need to encourage our guests to leave reviews and we need to ensure they're good ones by giving gold standard customer service."

"Tell that to the people who had their cars blown to pieces or the ones who wound up in the emergency room." Emily twirled her earring in her ear as she narrowed her gaze on Deanna.

José slammed his fist on the table. "The fish was not our fault! Neither were the cars."

"Look who's talking, the man with the devil horns." Emily rapped the end of her pencil against her notepad.

Astonished at Emily's change in behavior as she'd always been so polite, Deanna fixed her with a stern glare. "Let's not get personal."

Emily swiveled in her chair to look at her. "He scares the guests, especially the children. There should be a dress code."

Touching the point of one of his horns, José frowned. "They're permanent implants. I can't remove them."

"Saw them off. Have surgery. I don't care how you do it. Just get it done." Emily pointed her pencil at the chef.

"Enough! This isn't your call, Emily." Even though her thoughts had mirrored many of those the head of security was spouting, she hadn't given it serious consideration yet. "After we hire an HR director, we'll discuss personnel matters such as this."

Speaking of an HR director, Deanna checked her watch. Her first interview of the day was due soon. She had to cut the meeting short. "Do we have anything else to discuss?" She went around to each manager and everybody said no, so she adjourned the assembly.

Only Chantale stayed behind with Deanna. "I take it that Emily and José don't get along?"

"She doesn't approve of him or anybody who's outlandishly different. They often argue." Chantale shifted the notebook she held from one arm to the other.

"I'm going to give it another shot to find us a recruiter and an HR director today. I'm also going to call the agencies to send over PR people. I don't think we can afford not to."

"Let me know if I can be of assistance."

"Just hold down the fort while I put on the HR hat. Don't talk to the press."

Their footsteps clacked on the highly polished marble floors.

Companionably they left the boardroom together then split off in separate directions. Deanna headed to her office and closed the door. Immediately she dialed an employment agency and asked them to start sending PR people. Then she called two others with the same request. They all promised to send candidates beginning the following day. She thanked them, poured a cup of coffee then settled in for her next round of interviews.

The phone rang and the concierge desk's name showed up on the display. "This is Brenna. Peter McKenzie is here for his interview with you."

"Please send him in." Mentally, she prepared herself for the worst while hoping for the best. She prayed it wasn't another whackadoodle. There had to be a few sane people in the interview pool. She only needed two. God, please let them show up today.

A strange sound tickled Deanna's ears, almost like a whisper or perhaps a wheeze on the floor but not quite. When it drew closer, she saw that a young man, in his late twenties or early thirties, approached in a wheelchair. He wore an impeccable suit, nicely pressed, and had longish dirty blond hair and a five o'clock shadow. Handsome, he offered a friendly smile and held out his hand to shake. "I'm Peter McKenzie but everybody calls me Mac. I'm afraid I can't stand. I was injured in Afghanistan."

Hurriedly, she moved her chairs to make way for his then returned to her side of the desk. A good feeling enveloped her as she regarded him, and she allowed herself to smile. "I'm Deanna Thompson, general manager of The Gilroy. Were you in the service?"

"I was a captain in the Air Force."

"Thank you for your service to our country. As a captain, you must have been responsible for many people."

"I was. Before I was in the Air Force, I worked as an HR recruiter for a few years. I'd like to get back into the field. I'll be honest, I was recently released from the Miami VA hospital for my injuries. I've been in there since I was shot down in Afghanistan, so I've been out of the work force for a year."

Impressed by his manners and his experience, she nodded and gave him a small smile. "I won't hold that against you. May I see your resume?"

He pulled it out of his briefcase and slid it across her desk. "I know my HR experience isn't the most recent, but I have a knack for hiring people and training them. I may not have use of my legs anymore, but I have a good head on my shoulders. I'm a very able disabled person."

"I can tell that by talking to you." She linked and unlinked her fingers under the desk, then made a snap decision. She liked him a lot and she wasn't going to risk losing him.

"I'm not an HR person but we're in need of HR people. I have a good feeling about you and I'd like to offer you the position of our HR recruiter. We offer a full benefits package after a ninety-day probation. What salary are you looking to make?"

Mac mentioned the salary he'd like to get and she agreed that it was reasonable.

Then Lynette and Graham tickled her thoughts, reminding her that she needed to let Mac know the hotel was supposedly haunted.

"Before we sign the contracts," she added, "I need to let you know there are rumors that The Gilroy is haunted."

Mac did a double take then laughed. It was a deep, pleasing, masculine sound. "You mean as in real live spooks floating around scaring people?"

She didn't know how *live* ghosts were, but that's what she'd meant. "Yes. Precisely. I don't believe the rumors, but several people do."

Mac scrubbed his clean-shaven chin and shook his head. "If I'm going to be haunted, it will be by the spirits of the men we lost to the war in Afghanistan. I reckon I can handle a couple more. Sounds interesting."

She had to agree with him there. Her life had certainly been interesting since coming to The Gilroy and trying to disprove the ghost theory.

They shook hands and arranged that he would start work the following Monday morning. He left with another handshake and a smile.

One down, two to go.

Teena called. "Your next applicant is here. Should I escort him in?"

"Please. Thank you." Knowing it was too much to hope for a slam dunk with two great interviews in a row, she did anyway. She was due some good luck after her horrible ordeal yesterday.

Teena escorted a short, wiry man with red, white and blue spiked hair into the room. He wore blue jeans, a casual jacket and gym shoes. He also wore a ring through his nose.

Trying not to judge the man on his looks, Deanna did just that. Berating herself, she smiled at him. "I'm Deanna Thompson, general manager of The Gilroy. And you are?"

"Logan Parsons. I'm here for the director of HR position." He shook her hand loosely.

No. No. No.

She'd promote Mac to that position before hiring this clown to be a director.

Give the man a chance to talk before making up my mind.

"Please have a seat and tell me about yourself, Mr Logan. What is your experience in HR? Have you been a manager or director before?"

"I ran my own consulting company and did all my own hiring. We had fifteen people."

Uh-huh. "What type of consulting company?"

"Computers." He wasn't any more explicit and his eyes shifted as though he didn't want to say.

"What happened to your company? I take it you're no longer running it?"

"When the economy took a downturn I had to run it part-time. I'll still run it part-time weekends and evenings and work here during the day."

Oh, she could just bet he'd be on the phone with his personal commerce a lot more than with The Gilroy's business if she hired him. "Do you have any experience working in an HR position for another company?"

"No. But I'm the best at everything I do. I have the Midas touch, ya know? You won't regret hiring me. I'll have your HR department humming along smooth as a baby's bottom."

She didn't even want to see his resume so she didn't request it. He had no qualifications and she was going to file a complaint with the employment agency that sent him for wasting her time. "Thank you for taking the time to meet with me. We have several other appointments and we won't be making a decision for a while."

"Oh. You don't want me." He hung his head, ignored her hand and shuffled out. "I know when I'm not wanted."

Feeling bad for him, she wished she knew what to say to make it better but she didn't, so she let him go. He wasn't behaving professionally. If he had been in the running, he would have blown it with his exit.

Once again, Brenna called. "Your next appointment is here to see you. Should I escort her back?"

"Yes, please. Thank you." Waiting impatiently, Deanna was so ready for this process to be over. She considered begging Mac to start right away and take over the recruiting but she had to get his drug tests and background check back per company policy before he could start.

Brenna escorted a petite older woman to her who was dripping wet, her short straight hair plastered to her head. Her nondescript dress lay matted to her clammy skin. Black little old lady shoes, thick trifocal glasses and double hearing aids hinted that she was up in her years. Black mascara ran in rivulets down her face.

Deanna handed the woman a couple of tissues to wipe her face and hands. Then forcing herself to smile at the job candidate, Deanna shook her hand and went into her spiel. "Hello. I'm Deanna Thompson, general manager of The Gilroy, and I'll be interviewing with you today."

Much to Deanna's surprise the woman gave her a very firm, determined handshake. "Hello, Deanna. I'm Amelia Nicholson and I'm very pleased to meet you.

Please forgive my slovenly appearance. My car broke down on the way here and my air conditioner stopped working. I'm afraid Miami is a scorcher without AC."

Immediately, Deanna reversed her first impression of the woman. She was a tiny, articulate dynamo. With pleasure, she motioned to the chair across from her desk. "Please have a seat and let me see your resume. Tell me about yourself."

"Well, I've been in human resources for twenty-seven years. I managed the personnel department for my last company for ten years until they recently went out of business." With a reserved smile, she handed her resume to Deanna.

When Amelia mentioned the organization's name, Deanna nodded, recognizing it. Then she examined the resume and was even more impressed. "You have a master's degree from FIU in HR management. And several HR continued learning certificates."

Amelia nodded. "Yes. I'd be happy to present them if you'd like to see them. HR is my life. I love working with people. I've done recruiting, payroll, training, benefits and management so I'm well versed. I think I could be a benefit to your company."

"Amelia, I think you'd be a good fit here. However, I have to let you know some people think our resort is haunted and we've had a few problems we're trying to work through."

Chuckling, Amelia beamed at her. She threw up her hands. "How delightful. The hotel has history and character. I'm willing to live with the ghosts if they'll live with me."

"Then I'd like to offer you the job of director of our HR department. I hired a recruiter this morning who will be starting next week. Would you also be able to start next week?"

"I can start as soon as we get all the paperwork out of the way—the sooner the better."

"We offer full benefits after a ninety-day probation. What salary are you looking to receive?"

Again, they were able to agree upon a salary and they set up a blood test and tentatively scheduled a start date of Monday. Happy with herself, Deanna stood and shook Amelia's hand once more. "I look forward to working with you. I'm new here myself."

"We'll do great, my dear. Don't you worry." Amelia patted her hand and gave her a small but assuring smile.

The romance writers began checking out, still disappointed that they hadn't seen any ghosts. Then the housekeeping staff had a three-hour window to prepare the rooms for a soccer league and a plumbing conference. They also expected a group of golfers for a tournament.

Deanna's phone rang, the screen showing that the concierge desk was calling. "Dee, it's Brenna. We have a problem with five-oh-one and five-oh-three. Housekeeping needs your help immediately."

Spinning on her heel, Deanna changed direction toward five-oh-one, which was in the third building. "What's the nature of the problem?"

"Sydney didn't fill me in. However, he would like your assistance ASAP. The guests won't listen to him. I've called security too."

Deanna passed through the breezeway, which kept rain off but let sunshine through, that connected the buildings. She looked out over the pools and the golf course at the clear blue, cloudless sky and wondered what could go wrong on such a gorgeous day. So far, everything had been working out well.

She called Sydney and asked, "What's the four-one-one?"

"What do you mean, boss?"

Holding back her sigh, she explained, "What's the problem?"

"It's sort of hard to describe, but basically, we have two rooms full of furniture moved out into the hallway and the occupants refuse to move it back in. It's blocking the hallway and creating a fire hazard."

Damn. Hotels attracted some real whackos. Even high-class resorts. "Tell them they *must* move it back in or we'll ask them to leave immediately."

"I told them but they're ignoring me."

"Has security arrived?" Increasing her step to a power walk, she was almost running. Anger infused her and she counted to ten to keep from spouting.

"Not yet."

"I'm on the way. ETA is two minutes." Hopefully less. "Why did they move the furniture into the hallway?"

"Some kinky shit, I think."

Not expecting Sydney to say anything of the sort, she started coughing so hard she almost choked. She tried to get hold of herself. Meanwhile, she put her hand over the phone receiver to muffle her coughs.

"You okay, boss?"

"I'll..." —cough— "be..." —cough— "fine." Cough. Damn! She was dying. As soon as she reached a water fountain, she took a long, cool drink to soothe her throat. Luckily, it eased her fit.

A moment later, she reached the hallway in question and viewed the debacle for herself. The security guard showed up right after her.

Loud music and human screams oozed out of the room.

Shaking her head, growing more infuriated by the moment, she took inventory of the furniture, frowning at several large ugly dents and scratches she was sure hadn't been there before, as they wouldn't permit such furnishing in their luxurious rooms.

"Follow me." She grimaced to her staff. With the tall burly guard and Sydney by her side, she pounded on the door. "This is the hotel general manager Deanna Thompson. We need to speak to you *now*."

No one answered. After knocking again without success, she used her room key and tried to open the door. The dead bolt was set so they couldn't enter. She rapped on the door as loudly as she could one last time and raised her voice. "You can either speak to me or to the police. I'm giving you one minute to open the door or I'm going to summon them."

Finally, a woman with large bags under her eyes, an obvious cheap blonde wig sitting askew on her head and a cigarette dangling from her ruby-red lips opened the door. She wore only panties and a camisole that exposed most of her breasts. "We paid you for this room so stop pestering me and get out of my damned sight."

When the guest tried to slam the door in their face, the security guard stopped it with his beefy hand.

Praising him silently, Deanna made a mental note to give him a couple of lottery tickets after resolving this matter. "You signed a contract that states you cannot disturb or endanger our other guests, or damage our property. Not only are you being loud and obnoxious, you have endangered the safety of our other guests by blocking fire exits, other guests' rooms and the hallway in general. You have stacked our furniture causing dents and scratches, for which you will be held liable and charged. I want you out of this hotel within the hour. Do you understand me?"

"Go to hell. You'll have to carry us out bodily to get us to leave. And if you try to charge our credit card for the made-up damage to your tacky furniture, you'll be hearing from our attorney."

It wasn't the first time and it wouldn't be the last that she'd have to throw unruly guests out of her hotel. That was why she had the local police on speed dial. "Have it your way. We'll have the police evict you and we'll be pressing charges for all damages. Have a good day."

With that, she turned on her heel and left. Her nerves thin as a soap bubble, she clenched her fists at her side. After the unpalatable guest closed her door, Deanna called the police and requested their assistance to eject the guests. Then she instructed Sydney to have his crew remove the furniture to their storage area before they were written up for a safety violation—preferably before the police arrived.

As she made her way to the main building, she rounded a corner and literally ran into Harry. Bumping into his hard chest, she bounced back a step. Unsteady on her feet, she tilted before he reached out and steadied her.

"Whoa! Where's the fire?" He did a double take and softened his voice. "Is everything okay? You don't look so hot."

She chastised herself for her moment of weakness. Distasteful guests were all part of the business. "Just a wrinkle in the day. I had to call the police. They should be here momentarily to help us turn out some disorderly guests."

"I was coming to find you. When you're finished with them, do you think you can spare some time for me? I want to show you some things in room three-sixteen."

Quickly, she mentally checked her afternoon schedule. Amazingly, it was clear, so she said, "Okay. I'll meet you in there. I don't know how long this will take. At least half an hour."

"I'll be waiting." He turned and whistled a jaunty little tune as he headed back to three-sixteen.

* * * *

It had been over an hour since Deanna had said she'd come up to the room to see what he wanted to show her. Everything was ready so he played on his computer, which was set up at the round table in the corner of the room.

The outside light was causing a glare on the computer, so he closed the gold-trimmed brocade curtains and turned on a dimmer lamp on the bedside table. His feet sank into the luxurious plush eggshell-white carpet then he lowered himself onto the highly polished wooden chair.

When he'd opened Deanna's blog and found a new entry, he'd tried to swallow the grin spreading across his face like a damned inflating balloon. After he'd read it for the second time, he desperately needed a cold shower. His dick kept swelling and it would be mighty embarrassing if she found him in this condition.

Should he admit that he'd found her blog? Or should he keep it to himself and hope that she added more entries? It was so hot he was about to strip naked and ice himself down. So she liked him? A lot.

He liked her too. A lot.

Damn but she made him hot. That kiss they'd shared had been sizzling. He hadn't wanted to stop kissing her but she hadn't been in any shape for a roll in the hay and he hadn't wanted to hurt her. He cared for her too much to do her any harm. Maybe it was the car bomb, or maybe something more intrinsic, but he harbored a protective instinct toward her he hadn't had for anybody since his deceased wife Tracy, who had been gone now for fifteen years. He'd gotten into the ghost hunting business when she'd haunted him and he'd helped her to move to the other side.

What a hell of a time to think about Tracy when he wanted to get into Deanna's pants. As much as he'd loved Tracy, as much as he remembered her fondly, he was ready to move on. He wanted a future with one special woman. He wanted a family with kids, and a dog, maybe two canines. Deanna was still young enough to have a family

Damn. He raked his fingers through his hair and paced the room. Talking aloud to himself, not caring if the ghosts overheard, he said, "The woman drives me absolutely nuts. I can't stop thinking about her. I can't stop arguing with her and all I want to do is shut her up with kisses."

He pulled at his hair. "Ugh, what is wrong with me? She wants to have an orgy. I don't know that I'm up to that. I don't think I'm the sharing type." He'd always been 'Me Tarzan. You Jane. You *all* mine and *only* mine.' Hopefully it was a fantasy she didn't actually want to fulfill.

Now he could carry out the other dream, the one where they made out on a Miami beach in front of other people—as long as he wore very dark sunglasses and a baseball cap. She was due a day off sometime, right? He'd find out when that was, kidnap her, take her to the nude beach and see if she'd play along.

He couldn't wait to make love to her. The way her tight little ass bounced around as she jogged from one end of the hotel to the other made him so hot and horny he couldn't stand it. If only she was coming to this hotel room for some afternoon delight instead of a business consultation he'd be in seventh heaven.

A knock on the door interrupted his reverie. "It's Deanna. Sorry it took me so long to get here. Can I come in?"

His heart skipped several beats. He reached the door in three long strides and opened it wide to allow her entry. He drank in her loveliness and gulped. She didn't seem to realize how beautiful she was, which made her all the more attractive. "Please do. I've been waiting."

She looked up at him through her long, black lashes, almost coyly. "What did you want to show me?"

He closed the door so that nosy onlookers couldn't peer inside. "I want to show you the readings I've been finding. They're very high in here, so there are definitely otherworldly presences. Since this is the room where Lynette Cambridge stayed, I'm guessing she's our ghost. However, the reading is so high I'd say we have at least two ghosts. Her boyfriend is probably the second one." He pointed to his thermal readings, willing her to understand.

Squinting, drawing her eyebrows together, she leaned over the machine. "I don't understand what this means."

Prepared to instruct her, he showed her a normal, non-paranormal reading where the indicators drew a straight line. "See? When it's ordinary, it stays steady." Then he showed her this morning's readings that were still on the machine. "When there's psychic readings, the indicators are erratic. It's as if the particles are scattered, then coalescing, then diffusing again."

An a-ha light pierced her eyes. She straightened and hitched up her chin, staring at him squarely. "You mean like a ghost floating or flying? Appearing and disappearing? Like that thing I saw in the bowling alley?"

Excited that she was starting to understand, he wanted to clap. Of course he didn't, but allowed the smile tugging at his lips to come out. "Just like that."

She hooked her thumbs in her belt loops and regarded him curiously. "I've been wondering how you got started in this business? I mean, it's a little out of the ordinary."

Caught by surprise, he opened his mouth but no sound came out so he closed it again. He wasn't prepared to discuss his deceased wife with the woman he was hoping to score with. Not at this precise moment anyway. Then again, if he wanted to start a relationship, he had to tell her about Tracy sometime. Finally he admitted, "I'm a widower and my wife, Tracy, was haunting me."

Deanna's eyes grew round as nickels and almost as silver. "She actually haunted you? Why?"

"She needed my help to cross over. Just as I think your Lynette and Grant need our help to leave this place. Sometimes ghosts get stuck."

She rocked back and forth on her heels. She opened her mouth then shut it. A couple of moments later, looking leery, she finally asked, "Why do you think Tracy was stuck? Did something bad happen to her?"

Transported into the past as if a whirlwind had scooped him up and dropped him there, Harry could almost see Tracy's murdered body so clearly he almost smelled her, touched her. He did his best to keep himself from getting sucked into the quagmire of sadness that had overtaken him for the first year or two after her death. "Yeah. She was murdered. She couldn't move on until I solved the crime."

Deanna looked away and swiped at an errant tear. "I'm so sorry. I shouldn't have pried. So you have to be a detective and a ghost hunter. Do you have to be a counselor as well?"

Sorry that he'd made her cry, he wanted to take her in his arms and comfort her but he didn't move. Not yet. He didn't want to spook her. "Sort of. So our mission is to find out if Lynette and Grant were murdered and if so, how and who's responsible. I still bet sister dearest Roxanne did it, and from what I've seen and heard, she's one dangerous lady to cross."

"Well, let's do more research and look into it. Miss Roxanne wasn't exactly pleasant to me then my car blew up. What's wrong with that picture?"

"Agreed." He didn't like the *coincidence* one bit. He'd bet everything he owned that Roxanne had had something to do with Deanna's car exploding.

It would also be a shame to let a private hotel room go to waste when it contained such a beautiful sexy woman, so he moved closer and leaned against the wall beside her, letting his breath tickle her neck as he gazed down at her. He lifted a strand of her silky hair and let it sift through his fingers. Her heady scent wafted up to him, making him want to bury himself in her. Was it cherries? Maybe apple blossoms?

"My heart almost gave out when your car went up in flames and I saw you thrown back. I was afraid you'd been hurt... Or worse."

Her breath caught audibly, and she worried her lower lip with her small, perfect teeth. Then she gazed up at him with sorrowful eyes. "It must have reminded you of losing your wife."

"Not for a minute. I was worried *you* were hurt. That I'd lost *you*." He traced the line of her jaw with the pad of his thumb and shivered when she trembled. So she wasn't immune to him. Good. *Very good.*

Her lashes fluttered and her irises grew dark. She shrank against the wall as though unsure what to do next. Then resolution gathered in her eyes. "Oh! Well, uh, I should go. I'm sure I've been missed. A manager never rests."

To his dismay, she ducked under his arm and escaped to the door. When she tried to turn the handle, however, it wouldn't budge. Then she tried to turn the knob with both hands, pulling hard. Her eyes flashed fire. "What the hell? Can you help me? I can't get out."

"Do you really have to go? Or do you just want to get away from me? Am I that repellant?"

She looked as though she'd rather have fire ants crawl up her legs than answer his question.

Before she could respond, he jumped in, "I have a confession."

She stopped trying to jar the door, her attention riveted on him, her forehead puckering. "Did you do something I need to know about?"

Drawing in a long, shuddering breath, he look heavenward and crossed his fingers behind his back, hoping she wouldn't throw something at him, hoping she'd be okay with his admission. "I found your blog and read it."

She paled, the blood fled from her flesh and her eyes looked like sooty coals against her face. Her gaze clashed with his and held.

"How did you find it?" she questioned. "I used a pseudonym and I put it on privacy settings."

He screwed up his lips and scrubbed his hand over his face, preparing to tell more truths that were painful. "I'm a bit of a hacker and I like to research the people I'm working with." Not sure if she'd be receptive to his theory, he left out the part where he thought the ghosts had led him to her site. He thought they were closet romantics. He wouldn't be surprised if they'd locked them into the room now to force them into some alone time together.

When a tsunami of emotions flitted across her face, he tried to read them. Fury. Embarrassment. *Lust?*

"You investigated me? You read my private musings?"

"You wrote about me? In some very intimate ways. At least, I presume it was me since you used my name." He fixed her with a piercing gaze. "Did you?"

A pregnant pause filled the air as she veiled her eyes from his view. Finally, she smoothed her skirt against her legs and admitted, "Yes. I have very mixed feelings about you. You make me crazy the way we argue, the way you believe in ghosts, and yet I find myself thinking about you, fantasizing about you."

Taking heart in the last part, even if he wasn't sure he liked the first, he said with a lopsided grin, "You fantasize about me much?"

Surprising him, she sidled up to him with a mischievous twinkle in her eyes and ran the tip of her finger down his chest. "Aren't my blogs proof? The question is— Do you fantasize about me?"

He wanted to scoop her into his arms and haul her onto that king-size bed right now, and have his wicked way. The sooner they lost every stitch of their clothing, the better. Luckily, he'd started packing protection since reading her blogs as he'd been thinking about ravishing her, not that he thought he'd ever get the chance.

"I am right now." He lowered his head, smiled lasciviously and crooked his finger at her. "Come here, baby."

"I can't believe this is real," she said huskily. Yet she started to move toward him.

She glided so seamlessly she seemed to float. When she was within touching distance, he drew her into the circle of his arms, bent his head and captured her lips. He teased her with his tongue, seeking entrance to her mouth. He rocked against her, molding her curvy body to his. She was so warm, so soft. He wanted to lose himself in her.

Against her lips, he murmured, "I'm usually the one you accuse of believing in fantasy. Are we switching places?"

"Um. Maybe. Crazy, isn't it?" She kissed him back languidly at first, then with more fervor. She curled her arms around his neck and let her fingers play in the hair at the nape of his neck.

While she moved her hands north, he let his travel south. He slipped his palms from her waist to her buttocks, cupping them. Then he crushed her to him, yearning to be one with her.

"Absolutely insane," he said.

"We shouldn't be doing this." But she didn't try to draw away, didn't stop rubbing against him, inciting him.

"Yes, we should."

Her nipples budded against him and she quaked. Her flesh heated and she couldn't stop kissing him. If those weren't signs she wanted him, nothing was.

He returned her kisses and let his hands roam her body. Eager to feel her naked flesh against his, he pulled her uniform top out of her skirt. When she didn't protest, he lifted it over her head and tossed it onto the chair. Her breasts were barely contained in her wispy, lacy red bra, the large mounds trying to spill out.

Unable to help himself, he bent his head and buried his face in her cleavage. He shoved one side of the bra off her areola and laved her burgeoning nipple with his tongue. When she moaned and craned her head back to give him better access, he reached around and unsnapped her bra, whisking it off her and throwing it across the room. She writhed against him, and he cupped her other breast in his hand.

Breathlessly, she asked, "What did you think of my fantasy?"

"It made me really hot. I say on your next day off we go to Miami, to that nude beach, and make out." He switched breasts and suckled the other nipple. Playfully, he nipped it and pulled it deeper into his mouth.

"I'll bring the sunblock."

Around her breast he murmured, "I'll bring the sunglasses and baseball caps."

"Are we really going to do this?"

Lifting his head so he could look into her eyes, he drawled, "This? Or that?"

"Both," she said huskily.

Her female aroma washed over him and he couldn't wait to be one with her. He pulled her skirt up around her hips, inserted his hand inside her red, lace-trimmed cheeky panties and sought the source of her heat. Harry tangled his fingers in the curls surrounding her pussy as he traveled farther south. When she parted her legs, he massaged her clit.

She moaned and unbuckled his slacks, then tugged down the zipper. Clumsily but with determination, she pushed down his slacks then his briefs until his throbbing cock sprang out into her hands. She curled her fingers around his shaft and pumped it.

It was his turn to groan. Wanting to make her feel as good as he did, he slipped his finger into her pussy, which was wet and warm and so ready for him.

Deanna moved one of her hands from his cock and to his balls. Gently, she kneaded them.

Wanting to be completely naked at her side and already within an inch of coming, he warned, "Keep doing that and I'm going to come in your hands."

"Ditto." The tip of her tongue peeked out, moistening her lips. "I'd much rather you come in me. Do you have protection?"

Panting, he said, "In my wallet, on the table." Impatient, so hot for her he was about to explode, he hated to stop their momentum but agreed that it was important.

"Get it. Now."

While he found the foil packet, she shimmied out of her skirt and panties.

He finished stripping then tore open the condom package.

Taking the rubber from him, she sensually rolled it onto his cock. Then she tugged on him gently, pulling in the direction of the bed. Winking, she slanted her head at the delicious-looking mattress.

Unable to wait another moment, he scooped her into his arms and tossed her onto the bed. Then he jumped onto it beside her, making it bounce. When she yelped in surprise, he pulled her into his arms and crushed her to him. Just as he'd imagined, she was a perfect fit.

"You're even hotter than I imagined. And I fantasized you as hotter than hell." She licked and nipped a trail from his shoulder to his nipples, then swirled her tongue around his areola. Next, she laved the other one as he trembled beside her.

"Back at you, babe." Ready to be one with her, he rolled her beneath him and thrust inside with one long, smooth stroke. He savored her tight pussy for a moment, then struck up a sensual rhythm.

When her hips met him thrust for thrust, her vagina clenching him tightly, he shot to paradise. She raked her nails down his back and the pleasure combined with pain pushed him over the edge. With abandon, he drove into her wildly. Finally, he catapulted to the stars.

A moment later, she screamed in ecstasy and clung to him. She reached up and kissed him. He returned the kiss, their tongues slow-dancing.

* * * *

When Deanna was in her PJs, yawning widely and about to slip into bed, her cell phone rang. For once, she wished she had the luxury of ignoring it. She was exhausted but well sated from the afternoon's delightful time spent with Harry. But she was on duty twenty-four-seven so was forced to take the call.

Every now and then, she hated her job and this was one of those times. Could she ever get a minute's rest? She answered the phone. "Deanna here."

Breathlessly, Tabitha said, "There's freaky activity in the bowling alley again. Pins started falling in front of the guests. Worse, they flew out and started flying straight at them, like they were going to attack them."

Damn. Like they did with me. "Is anybody hurt? The pins didn't strike anyone, did they?"

"I don't think so but the guests are hysterical. They ran out of the bowling alley screaming bloody murder. Other guests rushed in to see what the commotion was about and witnessed it too. Our workers George and Joel refuse to go anywhere near the lanes. They're threatening to quit. Several guests are checking out and demanding their money back for their stay. Should I comp them a night's stay, or what?"

Hating to comp rooms, she didn't see any way around it. If inanimate objects started chasing her, threatening to bash in her skull, scaring the living daylights out of her, she'd demand her money back too. "Comp them a night's stay and apologize profusely."

"Yes, boss. Will do." Tabitha sounded less than sure despite her words.

"Tell the lane attendants I'll be right there and for them not to leave." Groaning, Deanna tugged the bow on her kitty cat pajama bottoms loose, preparing to kick them off. She signed off, undressed, jumped into her uniform and tied her hair up in a high ponytail. Almost ready to go, she slipped on her shoes before calling Harry.

"I need you." She'd meant to say, 'I need your help', but the Freudian slip had gotten the better of her. "Can you join me at the bowling alley right away? Pins are flying around, following people again. At least they were until they scared everybody out."

"I'm on my way." Glee and excitement tinged Harry's voice.

Those weren't exactly the emotions overcoming her at the moment. Apprehension, worry and even some anger that somebody would dare endanger her guests and her staff strafed her. "Did you set up your surveillance cams like you were planning?"

"Of course. We should have some good footage to view. I almost forgot to tell you that we captured some video of knives flying about the kitchen last night, too."

Annoyed, pushing her hair errant behind her ear, she asked, "When were you planning to tell me?"

"I didn't want to disturb you after the rough night you'd had. You needed your rest and you were in meetings all day today. I'll show you when we view the bowling alley tapes."

Anxious to see everything, she picked up her step. Minutes later, she came upon the cowering George and Joel outside the bowling alley. As she was about to ask them for their version of what had happened, Harry showed up.

"What happened, guys?" Harry beat her to the questioning, staring at them with cheerful inquisitiveness.

Hugging himself, shaking and shifting his weight from one foot to the other, the young pimply-faced George said, "Really freaky shit. Pins started falling on turned-off lanes. Then all of a sudden, they started to fly out and chase the bowlers. People were running and screaming. It was utter pandemonium."

"Did anybody get hit by a pin? Did you see any ghosts or shimmering clouds?"

The second young man, a nerd with black horn-rimmed glasses taped together and pens in a pocket protector of his white button-up shirt, slipped an asthma inhaler out of his pants pocket and puffed on it. Then he spoke in a rather high-pitched voice. "The pins started pursuing us, acting like they were going to smash in our skulls. I didn't see strings or anything holding up those pins. They were really flying on their own—or being held up by ghosts—I swear it! They stopped as soon as we left the bowling alley. Once we were out, the doors slammed shut behind us as if something wanted to be alone in there. It still sounds like somebody's bowling, but all the customers left."

George added, "No, we didn't see any ghosts or shimmery clouds, just flying pins."

Harry tapped his chin with his forefinger. "Sounds like we have an anti-social ghost on our hands who doesn't play well with others."

About at her wits' end, she turned to Harry and asked, "What's your master plan, Obi Wan?"

"First, we'll view the tapes. Then we have to dialog with Lynette and Grant."

She blinked several times. "As in talk to the ghosts?"

"Precisely." Harry made a phone call and spoke low into his phone. After he ended the call, he took Deanna's elbow into his hand. "Bruno's setting up the surveillance video now. Let's go."

Deanna thanked the attendants, gave them each a couple of scratch-off tickets, and apologized for all the trouble. She sent them home. "We'll take it from here."

More than eager to leave, George and Joel skedaddled away, murmuring between themselves. They made a beeline for the back employee exit.

To Harry, she said, "How much do you want to bet me that they don't come back to work?"

Harry ran his finger around the rim of his T-shirt as though it was too tight and he needed to breathe. "If you were their age, earning minimum wage, would you come back to face a potentially violent ghost?"

"Put that way, probably not."

Shortly, they entered Harry's temporary office where Bruno waited.

"I've got the footage in question right here," Bruno informed Harry. "Let me know when you're ready for me to roll it."

After they were comfortably seated, Harry gave the go-ahead. "Let's see what happened to frighten everybody."

As Deanna watched the scene unfold, she perched on the edge of her seat and wrung her hands. Something weird was certainly up, ghosts or not. When they were finished watching, she asked, "Are ghosts the only explanation?"

"Other than full-blown movie magic, which would require a lot of technicians and equipment behind the scenes, I believe so."

Bruno stroked his Vandyke and added his two cents. "Stuff like this would usually be drawn with graphics in the movies."

Doggedly, she refused to believe that the only answer was ghosts. "We have to keep digging. We have to catch the guilty parties."

"We will." Harry reached over and squeezed her hand then didn't release it.

Bruno acted as if he didn't notice the endearment but Deanna's face still burned. Despite that, she didn't withdraw from his embrace.

* * * *

The next day the concierge desk's name showed on her phone's caller ID and Teena's raspy voice greeted her after she answered the call. "Sorry to bother you, Dee, but we have a problem with the high school kids."

Deanna's gut clenched and the beginnings of a headache pressed against her skull. 'Problem' and 'high school kids' were never good terms to use in the same sentence. "You mean the soccer teams who checked in yesterday afternoon? What's the skinny?"

"Well, we think they're responsible, but we can't be sure. Perhaps if we run the security tapes…"

Counting to ten, tapping her toes, Deanna tried to hold her tongue and wished Teena would spit out what she wanted to say. Exasperated, she switched her phone to her other ear and settled on the arm of her La-Z-Boy lounger. "What's wrong?"

"There's total chaos on the third floor. Someone switched the room numbers. None of the numbers is on the right door. Yaniv has confirmed this with our master schematics. People can't get in their rooms. The wrong guests are trying to get into other people's rooms. People think room invasions are going on. It's world war three up there."

Great. Her headache grew worse and visions of people running helter-skelter through the hallways filled her mind. "What floors are the soccer teams on?"

"Four and five. But this is a kid-type prank. I'd bet my right ear they did it."

Just to be fair, Deanna didn't want to jump to conclusions. There were other groups in the hotel that could be responsible. "Not the Star Trek Con nerds?"

"Not their style. They're a little weird but more mature than that."

Deanna wondered about that but held her tongue. She could practically see Teena's head shaking in her mind's eye. She had to agree that it sounded like a childish prank. Her first priority was restoring order and proper room numbers to the correct doors. "Thank you, Teena. I'll take it from here."

As soon as she hung up, she called Emily Spencer and conferenced in Sydney and Yaniv, the engineer. "Do we have a schematic of the room numbers? Some pranksters switched the numbers on all the third-floor doors. We have to get up there and restore order immediately. Emily, please send up as many security guards as we have available. I'm told it's complete pandemonium. I'll be there in a jiffy."

Within minutes, she stood in the middle of the bedlam, her ears ringing from the screaming.

An older woman with a wide hairband, short dark hair, and a large ugly mole on the right side of her face ran up to her, crying. She grabbed Deanna's arm and her ragged nails dug into her flesh. "Strangers are in my room and won't let me in. You have to call the police now. They're stealing all my valuables, violating my privates."

A young, preppy bald man with a beard and mustache stomped up to her with murder in his eyes and interrupted, "My room key isn't working. None of our room keys are working. Your concierge desk printed me a new one and it still isn't working! What kind of hotel is this?"

Two policemen in blue uniforms arrived at the same time as the hotel security guards.

The younger of the two cops asked, "Is the manager here? We were called about room invasions for rooms three-eighteen, three-twenty-three, three-twenty-seven, three-forty and three-fifty-five. What are all these people doing in the hallway?"

Annoyed that the police were here to complicate matters but understanding why the guests had called them, she took them aside. "I'm the general manager, Deanna Thompson. There were no room invasions. What we have here is a prank, probably by a group of high school students. All the room numbers have been changed. I was just informed about this and we're preparing to restore the appropriate numbers to the right rooms and get everybody straightened out. I'm sorry you were called out about this. Our hotel security will handle this."

The older, much taller of the two male police officers shook his graying head. He popped off his hat and stroked his thinning hair combed over to cover a large bald spot. "If I were you, young lady, I'd have a serious talk with the kids' chaperone. Either kick them out or put them on probation. You can't keep calling us out here for childish pranks."

"With all due respect, our hotel staff didn't call you. The guests called." Deanna straightened her back and thrust out her jaw. She didn't appreciate being told how to do her job, especially by people who had never worked in a hotel.

"Make sure you keep them under control." He fitted his cap back on his head and glowered at her.

"Yes, sir." She almost saluted, but didn't want to get a citation. Still, she bristled at their haughty tone. "As soon as we view the security tapes, I'll talk to the chaperones immediately after. I can't accuse them without knowing that they are to blame."

"Yes, ma'am. Have a good evening." The younger officer spoke in a gentler tone and tipped his cap before turning on his heel and retreating. "Please call us if you need police help."

Deanna nodded and thanked him.

A few minutes later, when no one would listen to her or the security staff, she instructed one of the guards to fetch a megaphone and a chair. As she waited for the items, she and the remaining security guards knocked on the closed doors, informed the people inside that they were with the hotel and requested that they join them in the hallway. Unfortunately, only a few guests responded to their summons.

As soon as the requested equipment arrived, she wished she was wearing slacks instead of a skirt but climbed onto the chair anyway so that she could see everybody. Ignoring the strange looks she received, she mentally quelled her nerves. Then she projected her voice as loudly as she could. "Attention, please. I need everybody to listen very carefully."

Questions were shot at her before she could say another word.

"What's going on? We demand the whole truth immediately." A middle-aged woman with silky blonde hair shook her finger in the air at Deanna. A tall, young black man pushed his way to the front of the crowd, squared his broad shoulders and cocked his head toward Deanna. "Why are so many robbers and thieves in our rooms? I mean, not just in one of our rooms but also in at least twenty of them. What do you have to say to that? What's wrong with your security? We thought you were a five-star resort!"

Next, two plump, older women with graying hair hooked their arms together. They looked like they could be twins, even though one wore wire-rimmed glasses and the other didn't. Their outfits were similar with pink and blue kitty pajamas and plush, floppy bunny slippers.

The sister with the glasses piped up. "Why are people trying to break into our rooms? They're not quiet about it, either. You had to have heard them all the way down in the lobby. Why did you wait so long to send help? We could have been robbed at gunpoint...raped..."

Every time Deanna opened her mouth to talk, someone else interrupted. "Things are not as they seem..." she tried again.

"Then what are they? Why are you taking so long to tell us?" the other sister asked.

Frustrated, tense, Deanna almost strangled on the scream rising in her throat. "If you'll let me continue, we'll tell you what we know."

"Well, spit it out, girl! Stop dilly-dallying. We're tired and want to get back in our rooms and get some shut-eye. I have an important business meeting early in the morning I need to be rested for," a man, his hairline receding, spouted off. "Instead, you have us out here wasting our time."

Deanna bit back a sigh. Scathing retorts jumped to her lips, but she refrained from saying anything that would land her or the hotel in more trouble. The resort owners were quick to criticize and offer unsolicited opinions.

"If everybody will refrain from speaking and listen for a couple of moments, I'll explain."

Finally, the crowd permitted her to take the spotlight, and she breathed a sigh of relief.

"Someone has switched the numbers on the doors to your rooms. We don't know who or why, but we will view the security tapes and find out. At this time we have no evidence of robbery or bodily injury. If you are missing any valuables, if you have been hurt, please report to one of our hotel personnel who are standing on the sidelines with their hands raised."

On cue, her staff raised their hands to identify themselves. Not one of the guests made their way over to them. Indeed, some of the people in the crowd looked embarrassed.

Heartened to see this, Deanna continued, "We suspect this was a prank. Not a nice one and certainly not one we condone. Our engineering and housekeeping staff will begin restoring order and the correct room numbers on all the doors as soon as I finish speaking. We will—"

"You *will* compensate me for my stay here or pay to put me up at a better hotel for the rest of my stay!" a short, stocky man in a crumpled business suit yelled.

Other guests echoed him. "Mine too! If he's going to get a compensated stay, we demand it too."

Deanna's headache almost crushed her. She tried to ignore it and held up her hand again to motion silence. As soon as she could hear her words over the mob's din, she said, "We will comp everyone who is in one of the *affected* rooms for *tonight's* stay. We will make a list of the rooms involved and your bills will reflect the discount. If you have any questions, please see me, my assistant general manager, or one of our front desk staff and we will be happy to answer them."

"I still say you should comp our entire visits," the businessman said, pumping his fist in the air. "Some of these people were traumatized. Your security staff should have prevented this from happening."

"I promise we will get to the bottom of this, sir, and we will not let the people who did it get away lightly. If you would like to speak to me in private, I will be at your disposal as soon as we dismiss this meeting." She would gladly find him accommodations at a sister hotel down the road. If it would shut him up, she would gladly pay for his new hotel out of her own pocket.

Appeased, the man backed down.

As soon as they had calmed the guests, and Deanna had personally made other hotel reservations at a different lodge for the troublesome man, she joined the night security supervisor, Roger, in his office. "Show me the security tapes of the past couple of hours on the third floor. We need to see who switched those room numbers."

Sure enough, a group of giggling teenagers with screwdrivers had changed the room numbers. Some had acted as lookouts while the others had worked quickly. They appeared to be about sixteen and seventeen years old.

Next, she visited Teena, who was reading a bodice ripper novel. When she spied Deanna, she gulped and tried to sit on the book to hide it. "Hi, Dee. Can I help you with something?"

"Yep. I need the room numbers of the soccer teams' chaperones ASAP. Print them out for me." Godzilla couldn't be angrier than she was at this instant. Those chaperones were going to get a royal piece of her mind. If shit truly rolled downhill, those kids were going to be buried in it.

Moments later, Teena tore off a printout and handed it to Deanna. "Here you go."

"Thanks." Deanna returned to her office where she called all the chaperones and demanded that they meet with her in her office immediately. A couple of them balked, but when she told them to come now or check out of the hotel, they agreed to meet with her.

Finally, all of them were in her office, looking at one another as though wondering what was going on.

"I asked you here because some of the kids vandalized our hotel and caused quite a disturbance. It was so bad that several of our other guests called the police. We can't have this. If it happens again, we'll have to ask you to check out immediately."

Angry murmurs arose, so Deanna lifted her hand to quell them. "Specifically, a group of about ten teens changed all the room numbers on the third floor. Our guests on that floor couldn't access their rooms. Others thought their rooms had been invaded."

"Why are you blaming our children? What gives you the right?" A youthful woman with totally white hair looked like she was about to be violent to protect her young. Somehow, she managed to look fierce, despite her pink shirt and pink shorts that said 'Juicy' across the butt.

"We captured it all on video tape, which I viewed before calling you. I wouldn't accuse anyone without proof. One of the boys is wearing his school T-shirt. Buchanan High is one of your high school teams, isn't it?" Deanna lifted an eyebrow knowingly.

The woman who had spouted off swallowed hard and put her French-manicured hand to her throat. "He was? I want to see those tapes."

"So do we," the others said in chorus, moving closer together.

"No real harm done, right? No one was hurt. Room numbers can be changed back without damage, correct?" the white-haired woman asked.

Deanna pounded the flats of her hands on her desk, making some of the group members jump. "Wrong! We had to comp our upset guests a night each. I had to move one of them to another hotel and pay for his entire stay! We're out more than a couple of thousand dollars because of this *little* prank. It's not so funny now, is it?"

"We're not covering that expense. You didn't have to give them free nights. That was your decision and that's on your head." The white-haired woman lifted her chin haughtily and folded her arms across her chest.

The other chaperones followed their leader and nodded sharply too.

Narrowing her eyes, Deanna regarded the woman with growing dislike. "I didn't ask you to. However, if anything else untoward happens, we will demand that you leave and not return. The police are behind us on this."

"What makes you think we'd want to come back? You call this hospitality?"

Deanna tried to bite her tongue but couldn't. "You call what you're doing right now teaching your children responsibility? Or respect? Why should we welcome you with open arms if you're costing us money? We're a business, not a charity."

"You're heartless," another middle-aged man with a bald spot and an unruly mustache said. "They're just kids."

"Tell that to our other guests who were crying, who thought someone wanted to rape and rob them. How would you like to experience those emotions? Above all else, don't you want to feel safe when you stay at a hotel? You've destroyed that sense of security for those people." Infuriated on those guests' behalf, Deanna wanted to bash the chaperones' heads together to make them see sense.

"If you want to see the tapes, follow me. They're in the security office. We'll be happy to make copies for you."

They all followed her like little ducks in a row, still quacking.

Chapter Six

Chantale joined Deanna and Harry in Deanna's office the next day.

"When are you going to have a séance? We have to speak to the ghosts, see who they are, what they want," her second in command wanted to know.

That was all Deanna needed, a séance. Next, she'd have a dramatic clairvoyant in her establishment wailing and pretending to channel people who weren't there.

Cracking his knuckles, Harry pursed his lips. Then he said, "We should. The sooner, the better. I've been saying that we're going to speak to the ghosts."

"By that, you meant hold a séance?" Deanna did a double take. "You're driving me crazy again. Just when I think you might be sane, you prove me wrong."

Chantale gave her the evil eye and struck a miffed pose. In her pearl necklace and matching pearl ear studs, she managed to look refined and simultaneously fanatical. "Séances really work. I've been involved in many. I can help. Three of us will work, but a few more people, preferably believers, would be better."

"Count me out. I played with Ouija boards as a kid. Someone always cheated and pushed around the planchette to make it look like spirits were visiting. It's rigged, just like séances are rigged." Leaning back in her chair, Deanna linked her hands behind her head and looked challengingly at each of her cohorts in turn.

Squinting, Harry regarded her somberly. "Come tonight and I'll prove it's real, no hocus-pocus. Who else should we invite? My crew? Bruno and Keri?"

Bobbing her head, Chantale added, "They'll be good. And Sydney. He's from the islands. I'm sure he's a believer."

Frowning, Deanna sat forward and folded her hands on her desk. "I don't know…"

"Scared?" Harry's gaze dueled with hers. "I thought you didn't believe in ghosts and demons? If you don't believe then there's nothing to be scared of."

Growing more annoyed by the moment, Deanna crinkled her nose, and she itched to wad up a piece of paper and hurl it at Harry's smug face. Instead, she said, "I'm not scared. It's all hokum."

"So you keep saying, yet you hired me. You believe you're throwing away good money on my services?"

Ugh! She wanted to scream and tear out her hair. "You know I hired you to find the real perpetrators, to disprove the ghost theory."

"But I find ghosts more often than not. You may have hired the wrong guy."

Wrong guy… That depends on what he means by that.

"You *must* join us," Chantale said in her soft, but resolute voice. "You're our leader."

"She's right." Harry steepled his fingers before his face and peered at her over his hands.

Wondering if she was a fool, she relented anyway. "Oh, all right! If it'll shut the two of you up, I'll join you. Should we meet for dinner in the hotel restaurant at five-thirty then get the show started right after?"

"Sounds like a plan. I'll let Bruno and Keri know." Harry stretched out of his chair and his shadow fell across Deanna. He circled his shoulders as if working kinks out.

"I'll let Sydney know." Chantale fingered her pearls, moving them back and forth.

Looking heavenward, Deanna wondered what she was getting herself into.

* * * *

After dinner, Deanna girded herself for what was coming. If for one moment she allowed herself to believe in this stuff, then she had to consider the possibility that they could release evil spirits just as easily as good ones. Then what? So far their 'uninvited guests' did nothing scarier than bowl and cook. What if guests started showing up murdered?

On that note, she remembered the car bombing, and shivered. Maybe that had been an angry ghost, not Roxanne at all.

Stop this nonsense!

She tried to shake some sense into herself. She'd grown up watching *Scooby Doo*. The ghosts and monsters always, always, *always* turned out to be a live person, a criminal trying to blame their unlawful ways on the supernatural. Never once had there been a real ghost.

Of course, that was a cartoon...

But damn it, that cartoon made a lot of sense!

Harry believed in ghosts. Or had he wanted to see his wife so badly that he had made himself believe in what wasn't there? Was he delusional?

Together their entourage headed up to room three-sixteen with three candles, incense and an offering of food, their apparatus for the night. During dinner, they had decided that Harry would be the medium as he possessed the most experience in leading séances.

They encountered odd looks from some of the hotel staff but Deanna just smiled and greeted them politely, instead of letting on that she felt like she was heading to a firing squad. She wondered if this was what the owners had envisaged when they'd implored her to hire paranormal professionals to rid their establishment of the spirits.

Sydney had already had a large round table with six chairs brought in. They dimmed the lights then lit the candles and incense before placing them on the slab. Beside the glowing orbs, they set out the food offering before they sat and held hands.

The air was very reverent and they were so quiet she could hear their breathing even as she held her breath. Then Harry squeezed her hand and said in a low voice, "Repeat what I say. Nod to let me know that you agree."

Everybody nodded, including Deanna.

He continued, "Spirits of the past, move among us. Be guided by the light of this world and visit upon us. Lynette, Grant, we bring you gifts from life unto death."

With a somber intensity, everyone repeated Harry's words. They waited for several minutes and nothing happened.

Again, Harry said, "Lynette, Grant, we invite you to join us. Be guided by the light. We bring you gifts. We wish to help you move from this life to the next."

Once more, silence reigned except for the whoosh of the AC overhead and their staccato breathing. Deanna wasn't surprised but felt bad for Harry and Chantale, who put such store in this stuff.

A third time, Harry spoke. "Hear us, spirits who inhabit these rooms, whatever your names may be. We bring you gifts and invite you to join us. Be guided by the light. Speak to us."

Lights flickered. A rush of clammy air hissed over Deanna's neck, making her tremble. Both the electricity and the candles petered out.

A scream curdled in her throat but she tightly clamped her lips down on it. Instead, she crushed Harry's and Sydney's hands in hers.

"We'd like to ask you some questions. If that is okay with you, please rap once for yes or twice for no."

Deanna's throat constricted and went dry as she waited. She wondered how she could really know if it was ghosts or one of their party who rapped—if indeed someone rapped.

Moments later, one rap sounded like a gunshot, and she jumped. Her nerves stretched thin as floss. She waited for a second rap but none came.

Without missing a beat, Harry continued. "Is your name Lynette Cambridge?"

Again, one loud rap sounded. Conversely, two raps sounded close together.

Deanna crinkled her nose and her thoughts whirled. What in the world did that mean?

Apparently, Harry understood for he asked, "Is Grant with you?"

One lone rap hammered this time, so lonely, even desolate.

"Did you commit suicide?"

Two very loud, sharp raps shot out like firecrackers. Deanna bet the ghosts were angry and she shrank into herself all the while repeating silently in her mind that she didn't believe in specters.

"I didn't think so. Were you both murdered?"

Predictably, one hard knock sounded. Then silence.

Deanna could hardly draw a breath in the dank, palpable air. She was downright sweaty.

"Do you wish to speak through me?" Harry asked, his tone commiserative.

Surprise shot through her and her gaze riveted to the shadowy man at her side. She was glad he was holding her hand for he was her lifeline in the darkness.

A single loud rap ensued. Then Harry's voice reverberated. "Go ahead. I'm ready."

Quaking inside, Deanna was scared for him. If this was real, she wondered if it was safe. She couldn't tear her gaze from him but probably for different reasons than everybody else at the table.

"I am Lynnette Cambridge and my fiancé Grant Haynes is here with me as he's been since we were murdered by my stepsister Roxanne Cambridge. She made it look like a double suicide and paid off the authorities to look the other way. Now we're trapped here until we can prove her part in our deaths."

Deanna wanted this to be real. She sure didn't want to believe that Harry was committing a flimflam. Still, she hadn't seen anything she considered to be concrete evidence. The rapping could have been rigged by another person hiding in the room. Harry could be pretending.

Immediately, her heart twirled in her chest. God, but she felt disloyal. However, she wasn't convinced all this was real.

"Be careful of Roxanne Cambridge. She will not hesitate to murder again. You must get Officers Billy Curtis and Davy Vandenburg to confess that they covered up the truth or we will never be able to move on. Help us, please."

No more words came. Finally, the electricity and candles came back to life like magic. Deanna jumped, sucking in her breath.

"Thank you, Lynette and Grant, for joining us this evening. We will do our best to help you. We thank you for your information." Harry's hand lingered on hers even though he stood. Then he said, his voice as smooth as butter, "Everybody break the circle of hands and extinguish the lights. Let's rejoin in the hotel bar."

Chantale bent over and gently blew out the candles.

Finally, Harry released Deanna's hand and put his on the small of her back to lead her out. After they had exited, Sydney turned off the wall light.

Harry whispered in her ear. "What do you think now? Are you convinced there are ghosts?"

Recoiling at his question, she moved away from his hand. She'd rather not admit her doubts in front of the others, knowing how much store he put into his life's work. "I'd rather talk about this in private."

He stopped dead in front of her and blocked her way. He rested his fists on his hips and glared daggers from his eyes. Grabbing her arm, he dragged her in the opposite direction of the others before stopping. His nostrils flared and the corners of his lips twitched. "Why? You still don't believe?"

Caught in an uncomfortable situation, her heart ached. Needles seemed to poke her all over and she couldn't stand still. "There was nothing tangible to grab onto." She spread her hands wide and continued, "I mean…"

"You mean you think I'm a fraud, that I made that up. Thank you very much. I think this is my cue for my crew and me to pack up and leave. I'll send you my bill. However, you'll never solve your problem by closing your eyes and hoping it'll go away. By the way, you have a big-ass problem. Officer Billy Curtis is now Miami Chief of Police William Curtis. He was a rookie when this happened. Good luck getting him to confess that he threw the case. He rose fast in the ranks after the supposed suicide. I wonder why?"

She barely contained a groan while her heart ricocheted against her ribs. "What about the other one, Davy Vandenburg? Is he powerful now too?"

Why was she asking him these questions if she thought he'd made this up? Internally, she shook her head at herself.

"I don't know anything about him. You should research it."

Because he is quitting. She put her hand on his arm and winced when he shook it off. "Look, I'm sorry. I don't know what to think. I've always been one who needs physical proof. To be honest, I never gave much thought to ghosts. I thought ghost stories were fun to tell around campfires to scare the other kids."

He harrumphed and looked at her in disbelief. "That's your idea of an apology?"

Inhaling deeply, she craned her head and looked up at him. "I'm sorry. I never said or thought you were a fraud."

"But you think I made it up?"

"Maybe you were caught up in the moment? Maybe your subconscious was thinking all that and it came out…"

"Hell! I don't believe you, lady. I'm outta here." He threw up his hands and stomped away.

Painfully, she stared after him as he rounded the corner out of her sight. Part of her wanted to run after him and apologize profusely. The other part kept her feet planted firmly right where they were.

That was where Chantale found her a couple of moments later, wrestling with her thoughts, as if her feet had been nailed to the floor.

"I thought you and Monsieur Harry were going to join us? We looked around and you were gone. Is everything all right?" Concern pooled in Chantale's dark eyes.

Struggling with her emotions and with her powers of reasoning, she debated whether to confide in her second in command. They were becoming more than colleagues. A friendship was blossoming. Still, she decided only to impart a bit of the scenario. "We had some words and he's not happy with me."

Tsk-tsking, Chantale shook her head and put her arm around Deanna's shoulders. "You still don't believe, do you? What are we going to do with you?"

"The only thing I saw to make me pause were the candles coming back on. But I'm sure that could be some kind of trick. I mean, a draft could blow out the candles. Someone could have been in the other room doing the knocking."

"And Monsieur Harry could have been making up what the phantoms were saying. 'Tis not surprising he is furious."

Deanna wanted to bury her face in her hands. "No wonder. He's probably going to resign and we'll be back to square one."

"You can't let him! Go to him. Apologize. Beg him to stay and help us. I'd do it but you upset him so you must fix this."

Boy had she fouled up this time.

Her phone rang and she clicked it open. "Deanna here."

Tabitha said in a panic, "There are thousands of seagulls and sparrows in our parking lot. It looks like that old black and white horror flick! They're dive-bombing the cars and the pavement. Come quick."

Her eyes must have reflected her shock or perhaps her body language.

Chantale furrowed her forehead and asked, "What is wrong? Can I help?"

Since she had to go after Harry, she nodded. First, she asked Tabitha, "Do you know why the fowls are here?"

"It looks like someone threw a ton of birdseed all over our parking lot. I can't imagine why anyone would want to. It's disgusting! There's bird poop everywhere."

Her first thought was that Roxanne was pulling another nasty trick to bring down the hotel, but this didn't sound like a socialite's style. Rather, it sounded like another childish prank. "Thank you, Tabitha. Chantale will handle it. I have something else I have to attend to."

Quickly, she explained the logistics to her assistant manager and suggested that she call the grounds keeping, engineering and housekeeping staff. She authorized Chantale to call in extra help, even a cleaning company if required. How much was this going to cost them? She wondered if so many winged creatures in one place could be dangerous or just sloppy.

With visions of *The Birds* dancing in her head, she threaded her way through the halls to the office Harry was using, hoping to find him. But the room was pitch dark. Cursing herself, she tried calling his cell phone but the instrument went to voicemail. She left an apology that sounded inadequate and she cursed under her breath.

Since she couldn't track down Harry, she decided to help with the fowl situation. The closer she got to the door, the louder the cackle. When she rounded the corner, she bumped into a crowd gawking at the spectacle of ducks, egrets, pigeons, sparrows and several other varieties of flying animal fighting over seed littered across the parking lot.

Teenagers lounging by the outer doors giggled. Some were outright laughing, holding their bellies.

Aghast, adults surrounded her pressing in, stealing her oxygen.

A man in a Phillie's baseball cap and a plaid shirt exploded, "If my truck's a mess because of this, your hotel is going to pay to wash it!"

The man in a three-piece black suit with a metallic blue tie to his right threatened, "To hell with a wash, if my Lexus is dented from those freaks, you're going to pay the damages."

Next, a silver-haired, hunched-over woman with dull, gray, scared eyes asked in a wobbly voice, "Are we safe in here? Are they going to start attacking the windows and try to get in? I saw that movie *The Birds* with Tippi Hedren. Call the National Guard! Something's got to be done to protect us."

Out of nowhere, Harry appeared and cut through the crowd. As he'd done with the reporters, he stepped in front of Deanna. "No one's in danger as long as we stay inside. The creatures will eat their fill and leave. Then the mess will be cleaned up. After that, we can assess if there's any damages. For now, the best thing you can do is return to your rooms or have a drink in the bar."

"But my car—"

Harry squared his shoulders and jutted out his chin. "Should be fine. It has probably survived bird droppings before and will again."

Although she was grateful for his intervention, she wondered why he'd defended her after their blow-up. Also feeling impotent since he was doing her job, she stepped up to take over. "Mr DeVeaux is correct. We are perfectly safe inside. We don't know why or how the birdseed got here but we will get to the bottom of this. Meanwhile, we'll clean this up as soon as the birds depart."

The laughter stopped and the teens slinked away. She'd bet they were the culprits. Again, she had a date with the video cameras. Like it or not, they were becoming her best friends.

First, she found Chantale. She was sorry she hadn't handled this situation herself from the beginning. "It's too dangerous to send anybody out there. I hope you didn't. We just have to let the fowl finish feeding. I hope no one comes back to the hotel and decides to get out of their car during all this."

"Luckily, I looked first before I sent anyone out. It looks like a cataclysm."

Deanna snuck another look out of the window. Indeed, it did look like a horror movie. Winged creatures were everywhere, pecking at food, some fighting, some colliding and falling to the ground. She could barely see an inch of sky there were so many. Whoever had put out the birdseed must have spread a ton and done it fast or they would have been pecked to death before they could finish. She hoped they wouldn't find any bodies in the mess.

"Have the security guards break up the crowd and usher them to their rooms or one of the common areas inside," she said to Chantale. "Have Roger meet me in his office. We have tapes to view."

"*Oui*, Deanna. Immediately." Chantale hurried off.

Soon the guards were dispelling the mob.

"I'd like to come with you if I may. Then I'd like to talk to you in private." Harry's face was deadpan.

She wasn't sure if he should join her. Then she figured why not? "Okay. Follow me."

Eager to see who was at fault, to put this situation behind her and resolve it before the owners bit off her head again, she rushed to the security office. She wondered if it was a criminal offense, not that she was against kids. She'd rather hoped to have one or two herself someday. Single at age thirty-seven, however, her prospects were dimming in that arena. Still, she liked them—when they were behaving and respectful. She hoped it wasn't the soccer team kids. However, she wasn't holding her breath.

Roger was waiting with the tapes from the past few hours for the parking lot area. "This is the one you want, boss. It shows the perpetrators."

After she and Harry had closed the door and taken their seats, he popped the tape into the machine and played it on the TV.

When she recognized some of the soccer team kids, she clenched her fists so hard her nails bit into her palms. "I was hoping it wasn't them." Now she'd have to follow through on her threat to make them move to another hotel. It wouldn't be pretty but it had to be done.

Moving close, Harry whispered in her ear, "Did you really think it would be anybody else? I don't think it's Roxanne's style."

"No. I was just hoping otherwise. Despite what their chaperones think, I like kids. Not that they will believe that."

Harry gave her an odd look but didn't comment.

Apologetic and her head pounding, she turned to her companion. "Roger and I will handle this. Thanks for all your help."

"Talk to me for a moment in private first?"

Harry was so cute, so persuasive that she couldn't say no, so she got up and followed him to the hallway. To Roger she said, "I'll be right back. Just give me a couple secs."

Leading her to a quiet nook, Harry towered over her. "I don't know what I'm going to do with you, lady. I only know what I want to do to you."

Her breath caught in her throat and she asked in a low, husky voice, "And what is that, sir?"

"I can't believe I'm about to say this as you make me so crazy."

Perplexed by his words, she tilted her head and narrowed her eyes at him. "What do you mean?"

"Take you to that nude beach in Miami and bring your fantasies to life. You haven't had a day off since I've been here. Can you take tomorrow off? You drive me to the brink of insanity, lady, yet I want to be with you. I feel alive again when I'm with you."

"You mean because of the way we get on each other's nerves? How fervently we disagree?"

He moved closer, within kissing distance, stealing her breath. "Exactly."

She bit her lip as her gaze drifted to the parking lot where flocks of birds still fled and brave news teams tried to film them. Her nerves zipped and zinged and she longed to close the gap between them and cursed the throngs of people who kept them apart. "I doubt I can tomorrow. How about the day after, if there are no emergencies?"

Narrowing his eyes at her, he said, "Are you frickin' kidding me? Chantale can't handle a clean-up?"

"This isn't just a normal clean-up. We're going to have insurance problems, PR problems, and I'll probably have to meet with the owners. The day after tomorrow."

"It's a date." He slashed a kiss across her lips and, just as quickly, turned on his heel and jaunted away whistling.

Although it was brief and cool, electricity flared and her insides melted. Her nipples tightened, her pussy clenched and she wanted to melt into his body. She longed to spend the night with him, and flitting thoughts of chasing after him with the invitation crossed her mind. But she discarded them as Roger was waiting and she anticipated a long, rugged night walking the soccer teams to neighboring hotels.

From Roger's office, she dialed Tabitha. "Telephone the closest large hotels and see if they have room for *all* the soccer teams presently staying with us. Do not tell them what happened here. Let them know we're having some problems, but don't let them know the kids caused it."

"Got it, boss. I'll call you as soon as I have an answer."

Minutes later, Tabitha called back. "The Emerson has space and their rooms are about the same cost."

"Good job. I owe you a lottery scratch-off ticket."

"Thanks, boss!"

"Be prepared to do a lot of checkouts. Chantale and I will assist you. Please call her and tell her to join me in Roger's office."

"Will do, Dee." With that, Tabitha hung up.

A few moments later, Chantale stuck her head around the door of Roger's office. "You called for me, Deanna?"

"I did. We have to walk the soccer team kids. I viewed the tapes and they're responsible. I warned their chaperones after the first incident this would happen if there was a second." Deanna's head pounded and she tucked a stray tendril of her hair behind her ear.

As she took a chair beside Deanna, Chantale asked, "I hate to kick them out. Will the kids have their parents' credit card information on hand to book new rooms? Will they end up on the streets?"

"They have to learn their lesson." Deanna had to stand firm or look like an idiot weakling and risk more incidents that would put their other guests at risk.

"But was it *all* the children? How many were caught on camera for both events? Can we identify the ones responsible and just walk them?"

Deanna hadn't considered that and appreciated the power of a second mind. "That does seem fair. We can give the chaperones the choice to move just those teens responsible for the criminal acts or to move their entire group. Good idea, Chantale."

A smile blossomed on Chantale's face and she clapped. "Are we going to tell them now or wait until morning?"

Deanna checked her watch—it was quite late, so she decided to tell the chaperones now but allow them to remain until morning. "We'll let them stay until tomorrow but we need to speak to them now. Are you ready? Let's put on our fire retardant suits."

Although the chaperones blustered and carried on, they decided that one of them would move to a new hotel with the problem children and the rest would remain. All but the white-haired woman thanked them for their fairness.

* * * *

The next morning, nineteen soccer team teenagers and one chaperone moved to the Emerson Hotel down the highway. Then Deanna hired a clean-up firm and started working with the hotel's attorneys to straighten out the insurance mess. As most of it fell to the attorney, she was just a conduit. Still, she had to soothe a lot of ruffled feathers and hire a local car wash crew to come out and give complimentary vehicle washes to the guests whose automobiles had been soiled.

That appeased most of the guests. One man whined that they should pay for all his expenses including his two-week hotel stay. There, she had to draw the line. As expected, he stomped away threatening to give a bad review and sue the hotel for everything they were worth.

Since the morning settled down after that and the daily meeting was surprisingly short, Deanna escaped to the celestial white-on-white spa for a much-needed massage, mani and pedi. First, she undressed and enjoyed a head-to-foot massage for an hour. The tall, bronze-haired masseur, who looked like one of the romance novel heroes, had magical hands and she booked another session for the following week. Next, she had a soothing pedicure. Finally, she enjoyed a relaxing manicure. In anticipation of the next day with Harry, she shaved her pussy.

As she was feeling so refreshed and everything was going well in the hotel, she planned to have her hair trimmed and blow-dried at the salon next door. Unlike the completely white spa, the salon was trendier, done up in shades of violet and purple with a few white accents. Local celebrities who had their hair done here had gracefully allowed them to take their photographs then autographed them and permitted the photos to be posted around the walls. They fostered many hours of conversation for new and old clientele.

Wanting her head to feel as awesome as the rest of her body, she let them wash her hair and enjoyed their fingertips massaging her scalp. She had to bite back moans of ecstasy, as it was almost as delicious as sex with Harry.

Thinking about him made her squirm more and she couldn't wait until the next morning for their rendezvous. She tried hard to put him out of her mind, but it was a wasted cause. All she could think about was his sexier-than-sin smile, his sultry voice, his magical hands, his mind-numbing kisses…

"Is everything okay?"

"Yes, I'm fine. Why?"

"You mustn't have heard me ask you to move to the chair. I'm ready to trim your hair." Katie, the stylist, wrapped a towel around Deanna's head and held it.

Embarrassed, Deanna offered a small smile and took over holding the towel before she rose and followed Katie to her station. "Sorry, I was daydreaming. Your fingers are awesome."

It was Katie's turn to smile. "What do you want done today?"

Deanna explained the slightly different style she wanted then relaxed back into the professional's capable hands. While Katie snipped away, she enjoyed the soft pop music in the background and watched the other guests. She was glad they looked happy.

When Katie was done cutting, she asked, "Are we blow-drying today?"

"Yes, please." She didn't want to return to work with damp, tangled hair.

Unfortunately, halfway through the process, Chantale called. "Boss, I need your help with a problem."

"Can it wait another...?" Deanna looked to Katie who held up ten fingers. "Twelve minutes?"

"Certainly. I'll prepare the documentation, which will be in my office when you're ready. Just give me a ring."

Anxious, wondering what needed her attention now, Deanna tried not to fidget. At least the cutting was done so she wouldn't screw that up by inadvertently moving around. As soon as Katie finished and she paid her and left a generous tip, Deanna rushed to meet Chantale. She hadn't liked the tone in her voice.

Pulling her phone out of her pocket, she pushed Chantale's icon. "I'll be there in one minute. What's up?"

"I'd rather talk when we're behind closed doors. It's about one of our employees. There's been some misdoings."

Deanna felt like she was on the edge of a widening sinkhole that was about to engulf her. She hated it when trusted employees did something against company policy, or, worse, illegal.

Since Chantale was in her office, Deanna closed the door and took a seat. She pulled it close to her desk and leaned on the desk. "What's going on? Who are we talking about?"

"I didn't want to believe it. I didn't want to bring it to you until I was sure, but it happened again and I have proof." Chantale twisted the pearls around her neck, making red marks on her flesh.

Waiting as patiently as she could, Deanna tried not to rush her assistant. From experience, she knew Chantale would get to everything faster in her own roundabout way than if she prodded Chantale. So she just nodded and said, "Okay."

"It's Brenna. A guest made her angry so she charged her credit card for a lot of bogus charges. In addition, she made several prank calls to the guest's work and home phones. The guest provided phone records and credit card statements as evidence."

Deanna's throat constricted, her breath coming in tight, shallow puffs. Never in a million years would she have thought Brenna capable of such duplicity. Disappointment welled in Deanna's heart. She'd expected more of the young woman. "How do we know it was Brenna and not someone else at the concierge desk?"

"I pulled our phone recordings and listened in. The concierge staff know we have that capability. However, they tend to forget or don't think we use it."

Chantale turned the papers around so Deanna didn't have to read upside down then she sat back and waited while Deanna examined them.

Not wanting to believe her eyes, Deanna asked, "Can I hear the phone recordings too?"

"*Mais oui*. I have them ready as I thought you might want to listen." She clicked a few keys on her computer, turned up her speaker and pursed her lips.

Momentarily, Brenna's thinly disguised voice started berating the guest. This happened several calls in a row for a duration of several days.

"And this isn't the first guest she's done this to?" Deanna continued studying the troubling evidence.

"I hope so. I mean, I hope there's been no others. One is too many."

"Agreed." Deanna gathered the papers together. "Send that voice file to me and bring Brenna to my office. We'll dismiss her together. I understand the hotel usually gives one week's severance pay for each year of service. Her personnel records, which you have here, say she's been employed by The Gilroy for two years."

"Under the circumstances, we don't have to give her severance or sign off on unemployment benefits. I'm not sure we should. She represented our brand and is running it into the mud."

Gazing first at Chantale, then out of the window for a few moments as she speculated, she said, "We'll give her severance and allow her unemployment benefits. The economy's still tough. But we will only provide what reference we have to by law and nothing else."

"Agreed. I for one can't wait until the human resources people start then they can handle all this stuff and we can stop working so many double shifts."

Hallelujah! Amen! Deanna chuckled. "By the way, I'm taking tomorrow off unless the earth opens up and threatens to swallow us whole." Even then, she planned to keep her date with Harry. She had a raw, ragged urge to be with him.

"Good for you. Hopefully with that handsome Harry of yours..." Waggling her eyebrows, Chantale allowed mischief to twinkle in her eyes.

"He's not *my* Harry." She couldn't look at her number two without giving away the fact that she wanted him to be, or that she was planning to spend the day with him in a very sexy, naughty way.

"Maybe not yet. We'll see. Don't let the little things get in the way. True love doesn't come around often. Don't waste it." Switching gears, Chantale returned to businesslike mode. "I'll fetch Brenna now."

Deanna moved everything to her office and readied the termination paperwork. Although she'd prefer to wait and let Amelia handle this Monday, she was afraid that Brenna would create further liability to the hotel in between now and then should they put it off. Worse, if Brenna suspected she was about to be terminated, she could wreak further havoc on purpose—then what?

No. She had no choice but to end the woman's employment immediately.

* * * *

After such a distasteful scene with Brenna at her termination, Deanna required a distraction. She also needed a new bikini. As she didn't have any transportation and she didn't have time to hop a bus to the nearest shopping mall, she stopped at the hotel guest shop. She'd been told they were one of the best local sources to buy a swimming suit anyway.

"Can I help you? Are you looking for something specific?" Hilary, the sales clerk, approached her with a sparkling, helpful smile. She was a young, willowy blonde, probably in her early thirties with brilliant blue eyes and shoulder-length, flat-ironed hair. She wore a white linen blouse covered by a vest with a bright, tropical print and she adorned it with the shell jewelry that was for sale in the shop.

Pleased that her employees were sufficiently sales oriented, Deanna smiled back. "I'm in the market for a bikini. I'm told you have an excellent selection."

"Along the back corner with beach wraps, water shoes, sandals, beach towels and everything you need for a day at the pool or the beach." Hilary led her past shelves of touristy Florida T-shirts, Hawaiian-style muumuus, logo-emblazoned glasses, ashtrays, towels, books, videos, shell jewelry, key chains and loads of snacks and sundries.

This was only the third time Deanna had been into the gift shop and it was the first time she was here as a customer. A size seven, she honed in on the suits that would fit her, not that she'd have it on for long. Well, she'd wear it in Harry's car to and from the beach.

She ran her fingers lightly through the racks, noticing a bright orange European style bikini with long fringe hanging from the bra. Gold rings held the wispy panties together. Brown, white, tan and orange beads threaded the ends of the fringe.

Next, she happened upon a black bikini that reminded her of a miniature tuxedo. A large black bow rested upon the high-cut bikini bottoms. It would show a large amount of cheek. The top was another big bow, which conversely looked like it wouldn't show a lot of cleavage.

Then there was a white bikini with very big red polka dots. It looked like a granny's bra and panty set. Or maybe it should have been sent back to the 1960s where it belonged.

After that, she found a midnight-blue crocheted bikini with a bikini top where the strap tied behind the neck and macramé tied the cups together. She really liked the bottoms because the yarn extended around the hips in a fashion she'd never seen before.

There were so many styles her mind started spinning but in a good way. She wondered which one Harry would like best.

Not nearly done, she continued on her journey through the racks. Next, she found a white with orange lace G-string bikini. The top was almost as skimpy as the bottoms that would barely cover her almost D-sized breasts.

Worse, she found a bizarre pasty-type, emerald green bikini with clear bra straps and clear G-strings. They had several of the ugly things in different colors. Amazed, or rather a little shocked, she held it up to Hilary. "Do we sell many like this?"

"They're one of our biggest sellers."

"I haven't seen them around the pool." Then again, she really hadn't had time to spend around the pool. She was too busy to do more than glance out of her window at it from afar on occasion.

"Maybe they're used privately in their hotel rooms or worn at the beach, away from the children here." Hilary didn't look at all embarrassed and answered the questions with aplomb.

A light tinkle of laughter bubbled off Deanna's lips. "You're probably right. I hope no one wears these in front of our minor guests." She wondered if they should sell them, or if there should be a dress code for the pool. She'd have to discuss that at the next manager's meeting.

Curious to see all the suits in their inventory, she continued her sojourn. The next one was cute, not overly revealing or granny-ish. Colorful shells adorned the straps of the light pink bikini top. A pink and green palm tree design adorned the bottoms.

"We certainly have a large variety."

"We do our best to keep a big inventory. Many locals shop here too. And some of our guests order from us online."

Deanna's brow quirked. "Really? That's interesting." She still had a lot to learn about this hotel. She'd have to visit the different shops and entertainment centers whenever she had spare time. It reminded her that she hadn't spent any time in the casino or the childcare centers yet, so she made a mental note to do so. Maybe she could interest Harry in a little Black Jack tomorrow evening. It would be a cool, refreshing way to end a day under the hot, scorching Florida sun.

Finally, she decided to buy the dark blue macramé bikini. She added a beach wrap, new sandals, sunscreen and a floppy straw hat with a big, dark pink hibiscus flower on it.

She was as ready for tomorrow as she could be. So why were her insides flip-flopping?

* * * *

By the time Friday morning rolled around, Deanna really needed a day off. Brenna had made a big scene when she'd left, threatening to sue the hotel for unlawful termination and listening in to her phone conversations. Although Deanna knew the hotel was legally in the right and she wasn't scared, the whole thing had been utterly draining. She also made it a point to remind the remaining employees that they could and would listen to their phone conversations for quality control purposes.

Even though the kitchen staff had reported mysterious dishes showing up in the mornings, nothing had shown up today.

She hadn't seen Harry all day Thursday. Usually she bumped into him at least a couple of times. She hadn't realized how much she looked forward to that until now.

The night before, she did a little research of her own, looking up Tracy DeVeaux's murder. She found out that what appeared to be a simple snatch-and-grab gone wrong had really been to cover up something much more dark and sinister. Tracy had been a policewoman who had uncovered political corruption in her department. When she'd been about to expose it she'd been murdered to keep it hidden.

Grieving, her husband had insisted her ghost had visited him and led him to her murderers and the corruption running rampant in the department. No one could deny that he'd solved the mystery. Some agreed that he'd seen Tracy's ghost. Others didn't. It was irrefutable, however, that the whole ordeal had kick-started his paranormal investigations company.

Her flesh tingling, she had woken up early, soaked in the tub with lavender-scented bubble bath, shaved her legs and underarms and pumiced her feet. Glad she'd had the manicure and pedicure, she didn't have to worry about her hands and feet. That gave her more time to work with blow-drying her hair and fixing her makeup to look casual but gorgeous—not an easy thing to do.

Afterward, she grabbed a yogurt, banana and some orange juice for breakfast, even though she was too nervous to eat. However, she knew she'd be starving by noon and might pass out in the heat if she didn't get some fortification.

By nine a.m. she was staring at her phone, willing him to call and say he was here. Instead, there was a knock on her door. Careful about room invasions, she looked out of the peephole. When she didn't see anybody, she called out, "Who is it?"

"Harry. Come to collect my lady."

Tremors skipped up her spine and she fumbled to open the door. Drawing it wide, she invited, "Please come in for a moment. I'll just grab my things."

Like her, he wore swimming trunks covered by a white terry cloth beach wrap. Bamboo sandals shod his feet. Very hairy legs stood out against too-white flesh. Now that she was more at ease with him, she had to tease him.

"You mustn't spend much time outside? Your legs are really white."

"Well, not in just shorts. Most of the time my work keeps me inside. Ghosts don't spend much time outdoors."

She gathered her beach bag, made sure she had a little money, locked her wallet in her safe and added her brush, lip-gloss and some hair ties to the bag. She didn't have housecleaning do her room. She cleaned for herself.

After donning her floppy hat, she rejoined him. "So you're saying you're a workaholic?"

"Like someone else we both know and love." A lopsided grin split his gorgeous face.

Her insides turned to mush and she wondered if he was just repeating an expression or really meant the 'and love' when referring to her. Could people really fall in love in under two weeks? They *had* spent a lot of time together…

Mentally, she shook her head. She was being silly. Today was about having fun and fulfilling a fantasy, not about romance. Couples didn't go to a nude beach to woo. They went to soak up sun and have sex—emphasis on the sex.

"I'm ready if you are." She waited for him to leave then locked the door. She led the way, waltzing ahead of him.

"I like the view already." A roguish growl rose in his throat.

The earth shifted beneath her feet as if they were on two different tectonic plates and she was about to fall in a deepening crevice and drown. Making sure the hallway was empty, she got her emotions in check before turning and flicking him with her beach towel. When he returned the favor, she was surprised. "This is war, but it'll have to continue at the beach." She couldn't have guests and staff seeing her behave like this.

"You started it."

Indeed, she had. She was finding out that being general manager was too much pressure.

Within moments, they were outside in the bright south Florida sun and strolling on a sparkling clean parking lot toward Harry's Jeep. Only a couple of egrets sauntered across the lawns, a far cry from the scene a couple of days ago. Few clouds marred the clear blue sky and glossy green palm trees lined the horizon.

"We picked a gorgeous day." Deanna exulted in being with Harry and couldn't wait to escape from the tensions of managing the city-like hotel. With the yoke temporarily off her shoulders, if only for a few hours, she was carefree and giddy. She wanted to twirl around like a little girl. Maybe she would when they reached the beach.

Harry squinted up at the bright sky that held only a few white fluffy clouds floating languidly, morphing from a scary dragon-looking creature to a cute fluffy-tailed rabbit. "It's Florida. It rains just about every afternoon. Let's get going so we can enjoy as much beach time as possible."

She swatted away a pesky mosquito almost the size of a hornet then, shaking her head, she said, "The weather report stated there was little chance of rain today."

Chuckling, Harry regarded her as if she was extremely naïve. "Like I said, it's Florida. Don't listen to them. I'll stop believing in ghosts when the weather men start getting forecasts right."

She had to laugh as she clambered into his steaming-hot vehicle and gingerly adjusted her scorching-hot seatbelt, careful not to let her fingers get burned on the oven-hot metal. She wondered if she'd ever get used to the endless summer and unbelievably hot weather. For God's sake, it was autumn! When was somebody going to tell South Florida? Then again, she looked forward to going to the beach and getting nude, something she never would have dreamed of back home in Vermont at this time of year. Hopefully Harry was wrong about the weather changing for the worse later, but in case he was right, she was eager to get going so they could enjoy their illicit tryst.

Her pussy clenched as she thought about their special date and she squirmed against the seat. Although perspiration dripped down her back and between her breasts, she tried to cool her thoughts. She forced her mind off sex and onto business. "Have you any other clients right now?"

"A couple of jobs are waiting in the wings for when I'm finished investigating your situation. They're not as urgent, though. No one is blowing up cars or making death threats. Just normal hauntings."

Normal hauntings? What a conundrum.

She twisted to look him squarely in the face and arched an eyebrow. "Is there such a thing as a *normal* haunting?"

He closed his door, inserted the keys into the ignition and started the engine before moving out of the parking space. After he fiddled with the control panel, a whoosh of AC blasted out and started cooling the vehicle. "Yeah, there are average ghost sightings. They're spirits that haven't been able to move on for a lot more mundane reasons than murder. Your haunting is only the third I've dealt with where murder was involved and I've been doing this for over a decade."

For some reason, she breathed a sigh of relief. She was glad he wasn't always in mortal danger but then she cut off her thought so she wouldn't have to examine the reason why too closely. She let the subject drop and watched his capable, sexy hands as they stroked the steering wheel. The unbidden thought came that she couldn't wait to feel those hands caressing her. Again, she tried corralling her thoughts over to a safer subject.

Harry had one of those reverse cameras that she wanted on the next vehicle she purchased. He stared into it before backing up. She'd love to have all the fancy bells and whistles, but didn't know if she could afford them. However, the backup camera was a requirement. Which reminded her... She needed to go automobile shopping. Not her favorite thing to do but a necessary evil.

"Do you know a lot about cars?"

"A bit. I do a bit of tinkering on my Jeep to keep her running when I have to, but it's not my favorite hobby. Why?"

Should she ask for a favor? They had made love once, and today would make it twice, but they hadn't exactly escalated to a real relationship. He was still her contractor, she his client. Still, whom else could she ask to help her buy a car? No one else at The Gilroy struck her as knowing anything about vehicles. "I need to buy a new car. Mine's been totaled."

He took his gaze off the road long enough to give her a commiserative look.

"My brother used to help me buy cars. He always said that car salesmen think they can scam a lone woman when she walks in."

He pulled onto the main road and slipped into the flow of traffic. Parking lots were overflowing at the local breakfast joints with cars sporting license plates from all over the nation, as they passed. Motorcycles and cars towing boats keyward-bound clogged the southbound lanes. Luckily, they were headed north to Miami so traffic was a little lighter on their side of the road.

"Would you like some help? If you like, we can look after the beach."

"I'd love to but I didn't bring my license." Plus they weren't dressed for car shopping.

"We can change before we go. Do you have any idea what type of vehicle you want?"

This certainly wasn't the foreplay she'd anticipated to their big fantasy, but it was productive. One to go with the flow, she checked out his ride again and ran her hand over the smooth leather dashboard. "I really dig your Jeep and I wouldn't mind having one myself. Of course, having a car payment will suck."

"Maybe you'll get a large insurance settlement and can pay a big chunk down."

"They only want to give me four thousand. I'm looking at twenty thousand minimum for the new vehicle I want."

"If you buy, it'll be four or five hundred a month. If you lease, only a couple of hundred. You're a general manager so you must make a decent salary, if you don't mind my saying. And I imagine your apartment's included in your salary since you live at the hotel."

"True." But she worked her butt off for the hotel. Not only did she rarely get a day off, but she also usually worked double shifts. She was always on call. "I shouldn't complain. I've been spoiled. I feel bad I let my brother down."

"It's not your fault. You didn't blow up his Mustang. You weren't negligent. Thank God you weren't in it when it happened." He drove the car past street signs that thanked them for visiting Homestead and for entering Miami. "Much as you probably liked that car, a 1970 couldn't have had all the bells and whistles the new cars have. I imagine you'll enjoy all the new amenities you've been missing. I see how you've been eyeing mine."

Whether or not he meant that to be a double entendre, heat crawled up her neck. She hoped it wouldn't continue into her cheeks. Since they were about to be so brazen and risqué, she let her gaze rake over him, hot and hungry, as she licked her lips. "I like yours *very, very much*. Of course, I'd like to take it for a test drive."

"You mean a second test drive?"

Oh, yeah, it had been a double entendre. Pretending to be innocent now, she widened her eyes. "I've never driven your Jeep."

He reached over and squeezed her hand. "Brat. I'll be more than happy to let you test drive my Jeep, after you and me, on the beach…"

As if on cue, they came upon a sign that said— *Haulover Beach. Attention. Beyond this point you may encounter nude bathers.*

"This is your last chance to turn back." He paused the Jeep at the neck of the parking lot. "In or out?"

What a question! Again, she wondered if he knew what he was saying. Determinedly, pointedly, she said, "In!"

Although her sunglasses and sunhat were already in place, she pushed the glasses further up her nose and pulled the hat further down her head.

"That's not going to work. Plus you need to tie up your hair. Did you bring a rubber band?"

She pulled down the passenger side mirror on the visor and frowned. "Of course it will. It's big and floppy and hides my face from view and the sun."

"How am I supposed to kiss you with that thing in my way?" He reached into the back seat and pulled out a pink baseball cap. "Here, wear this instead."

Pouting she said, "I like my hat better."

"Just wear this one. Do you argue with everybody?"

"No. I'm used to people doing what I say the first time I say it."

"Um. We're both the big boss so we both want to be the dominant one. I wonder how well this is going to work." He backed his vehicle into a parking space by the white sand and turned off the ignition. With it, the AC died and the sweltering Floridian heat started seeping into the cab, fogging her glasses.

"For heaven's sake, it's just a hat." But he had a point. She wasn't used to backing down to anyone, except the owners, and the occasional irate guest.

He threw up his hand. "Okay! Wear your floppy straw hat but I bet it'll get in the way. And it won't want to stay on while we're getting *frisky*."

Thinking hard, she looked inward. It didn't have a strap and it didn't fit as snugly as a cap. Then again, the large brim hid her face better. However, if the thing flew off or got in their way, it wouldn't hide anything. Decision made, she traded her hat for the cap, tied up her hair, and fitted the new hat to her head.

"Can I lock my phone and keys in your dashboard compartment?" As he did the same, she hoped his car wouldn't blow up too. Why that thought just now occurred to her, she didn't know. Which led her to wonder if it was safe to buy a new car before solving the mystery of how the Mustang had blown up.

Harry alighted from the Jeep, gathered their beach bags from the back, then helped her out of the vehicle. Bowing before her, he splayed his hand toward the beach dotted with bathers. "Your fantasy day awaits, baby."

Breathless, barely able to believe she was here and ready to fulfill her fantasy with her dream man, she pinched her arm. When a small red mark in the shape of her fingernails appeared that stung, she knew this was real.

"People really pinch themselves?"

His charming, mischievous smile was contagious and she couldn't help but return it.

"I do." To be honest, this was the first time she'd ever done this, which was nothing compared to what they were about to do.

"You're a conundrum. In some ways you're so matter of fact and straightforward, then you do little quirky things that catch me off guard."

If that meant she bewitched him, she'd take it. Hopefully, he didn't really think her dorky. He aimed his keys at the car and locked it, then he crooked his arm and motioned for her to put hers through it.

She really wanted to move into the twenty-first century and start living—a new car, a new lover, maybe a new relationship. All she'd been doing since her divorce and especially since Danny's death had been existing. She'd thrown herself into her work so that she'd never resumed a personal life. Of course it had paid off professionally, if being stuck working weeks on end without a day off, most of them double shifts, could be considered winning. For all the time and sweat she'd put into it, she could have become a physician. Still, she'd come a long way from her concierge desk days.

Underfoot, the warm, soft sand oozed between her feet and the bottoms of her sandals. The closer they got to shore the wetter and cooler it was and began to squish between her toes. Tiny shells crunched beneath her feet. Clumps of seaweed, stranded ashore, tangled around her foot so she had to kick it off.

Sunbathers in all states of dress ambled around the beach. A few were fully dressed in street clothes. Maybe twenty percent wore full bathing gear like them. About eighty percent were at least partially naked. Men and women of all ages and ethnicities went completely nude.

A group of young people played volleyball sans clothing. Their naughty bits bounced alarmingly as they ran for and spiked balls.

Harry leaned close to her and said, "That looks too dangerous for my liking."

"Yet you chase angry ghosts and criminals. I'd call that weird, not merely quirky, mister." She couldn't yank her gaze away from the players, many of the young college-age men well built, sun-kissed and gorgeous.

Harry cleared his throat loudly and pointedly looked from her to the volleyball players and back. "Call it what you will."

Understanding his meaning, she forced her gaze away from the naked young gods.

Seeking a spot to spread out their towel, he looked around. Then he changed direction and pulled her along. "Let's set up by the rocks. We'll have a bit of shade."

"Shade or covering?" She instilled a challenge in her smile.

Stopping dead in his tracks, he rounded on her and faced off. "Are you accusing me of being a coward? I'll show you." He set down the beach bags then shrugged out of his beach wrap, letting it pool at his feet. Then he pushed down his swim trunks and stood gloriously naked before her, white legs, creamy ass and all.

Harry threw up his arms and turned around slowly as if modeling. He called out, "Look at me, world, I'm not scared." He strutted down to the shore and back to the cheers of several admirers. When he returned, he took a big, sweeping bow.

Laughing, unable to take her gaze off his beautiful cock, she clapped. "You win. You're not scared." Now it was her turn, since the gauntlet had been thrown down. First, she removed her terry cloth wrap. Next, she reached around, unsnapped her bikini top and lifted it over her head. After that, she shimmied out of her bikini bottoms and twirled them around her finger. When Harry's eyes lit up with arousal, she was glad she'd forgone the bikini wax during her spa treatment day, instead shaving her private area.

"My turn to show off." She sashayed down to the shore, smiled at a few handsome young men and swallowed hard when their dicks swelled. Was she responsible?

When one of them pumped his cock in her direction and cum shot all over his stomach, she was mesmerized. Despite her better judgment, her pussy throbbed. Was she really having this effect on such good-looking, virile men?

A long shadow blended with hers and a primal growl rose over the sounds of the ocean waves lapping the shore and distant radios tuned to warring stations. A couple of men rose to their feet and started swaggering toward her.

Harry grasped her elbow and said in a gruff, angry voice, "Hands off, fellows. She's with me."

Heady with power, she turned and blinked at her wannabe hero. "I wasn't trying to attract anybody but you. I only wanted to prove I'm just as brave as you."

"Now you see what a beautiful woman you are and what you do to us men. Unless you want a ménage, stay close to me."

"Not today. You're all the man I need or want."

His cock began to grow and, fascinated, she watched it. Realizing how exposed they were to the elements, she licked her lips and said, "We should put on our sunscreen. I'll apply yours if you apply mine."

He craned his neck and looked up at the blazing sun reflecting off the white sands. "The sooner, the better, or this may be our final fantasy—for a couple of weeks anyway."

In a few steps, they reached an outcropping of rocks not far from the wet sand. It provided a bit of shade but not enough to go without sunscreen. She dug around in her bag and pulled out a large, new bottle of lotion. Holding it out, she opened the container and poured some into his hands, then she dispensed some onto hers. He rubbed the creamy ointment onto her breasts, followed by massaging it across her shoulders. After that, he moved lower to her belly, then her pussy while she rubbed some over his back. After that, he finished with her legs.

Not to be outdone, she applied the stuff all over him too, spending special attention on his cock and his tight ass. "Baby, you're so very tense. Unwind."

"Relax me." He rolled her to her back and lifted himself over her.

Thrilling to his touch, not sure she could hold out much longer before devouring him, she asked, "Did you remember your protection?"

He snapped his fingers in the air, teasing, "Wait! This is reality, condoms don't just appear in thin air?"

Crinkling her nose, she shook her head. "I don't think so."

"I thought maybe the ghosts took a field trip with us and would hand one to me."

"And I presumed you wanted this to be just you and me this morning. No ghosts allowed." She meant it. "You're all mine today."

"Okay. Bad joke." He climbed onto his knees, rustled around in his bag and pulled out a couple of condoms.

Sitting up, Deanna took one from him. She bit it open and reached for him. "This is my job."

"Be my guest." Long, hard and hotter than sin, he poised before her. Only a few hairs adorned his areolae. His flat abs and broad shoulders made her drool. Had she thought she'd seen men as handsome as Harry? She had been wrong. He was more beautiful than a Greek god, more stunning than a movie star and more delectable than a romance novel model. "You're the sexiest man I've ever seen."

"Ditto."

Although she knew what he meant, she had to laugh. She stood and turned around, modeling, holding her heavy breasts. "Since when do I look like a man?"

"Stop busting my balls, and start *busting* my balls." With that, he winked, yanking her down to him. He crushed her against him. They molded perfectly together, his cock fitting between her legs, tickling her pussy.

She snaked her arms around his neck and kissed him full throttle. They sank back against the towels, softened by the bed of sand. She plundered his mouth as he explored her body with his hands.

Wondering if anybody was watching, she snuck a glance and shivered to see that several gazes were following their every move. Against his lips, she murmured, "We're being watched."

"Isn't that what you wanted? Do you like it as much as you thought you would?"

"Oh, yes. Even better." This brought sex to an entirely new level. "What about you?"

"I'm a man. I like fucking you however, wherever and whenever I can. If this turns you on, it turns me on."

Close enough. So he was doing this to make her happy, or to be with her. Either way, she was flattered.

His tongue mated with hers as if they'd been lovers in a prior life and knew every inch of each other.

"I love kissing you. You kiss so soulfully." She pressed her lips to his with as much fervor as he was caressing her with. If opening the floodgates to her feelings was enough, she was going to drown them both with the depth of her emotions.

"I want you, baby—now." He lifted his hips and drove inside her, ramming her hips deeper into the bed of sand.

She matched his rhythm, meeting him thrust for exquisite thrust. His body rubbing against hers made her feverish, far more than the Miami sun could ever accomplish. Although one with him, she was more aware of her body than ever before, every nerve ending, every inch of flesh electrified. Breathless, she parted her lips wide to drag in much-needed air.

Hearing the commotion of a growing audience, her emotions amplified at least ten-fold. She soared to the skies, then launched into the heavens and beyond. When she realized that what really turned her on was the man making love to her, she suddenly didn't care if anyone was watching. They didn't matter. Only Harry did.

Against her lips, Harry muttered, "We're either going to get a Golden Globe nomination or arrested for PDA. Maybe we should have thought this through a little more."

"Then it's a good thing I'm coming. Ooh!" Clamping her vaginal muscles around his cock, she milked him until he also came.

The din grew louder and Harry kissed her tenderly, but briefly. He pulled out, helped her up and grabbed their things. "I think we should run and hide. Fast!"

She tried to look around to see if there was a law enforcement agent nearby, but he tugged her hard and pulled her behind him. "Why, is there a cop?"

"If there isn't, I'm sure there will be soon."

"Where do we run to?" Unfortunately, there was only white sand, water and people as far as she could see. No hideouts.

He looked around with wild eyes and changed direction. "Damn! Policeman at three o'clock. We'll swim in the ocean until we get down shore a ways."

She glanced around and saw the officer swiftly approaching with a deep frown etched on his face. *Damn.* "What about your car keys? Are they waterproof?"

"If we can get out of eyesight for a moment, we'll ditch our stuff, swim down shore, then come back when the coast is clear. I doubt our crime's big enough they'll chase us very long."

Crime? They were *criminals?* Her jaw dropped. She'd been so horny that hadn't occurred to her. Not on a nude beach.

She told herself to get over it and live on the edge. A little danger, a little fun, was good once in a while.

Tinkling laughter escaped her lips and she picked up her step, kicking sand behind her. "Is he still chasing us?"

Harry looked back and shook his head. "No. But I still think we should disappear for a while before making our way to my Jeep. Do you like to swim?"

"A lot." She'd been eyeing the hotel pools for weeks but hadn't had time to enjoy them.

"Well, today's your day. You get to frolic in the ocean." He dropped the bags, rummaged through and pulled out their suits. "Hurry and put this on. Take off the hat and glasses. We want to look as different as possible."

He took the hat and glasses with them and ditched them in the first garbage can they passed. He swept her off her feet, carried her into the ocean and, with a wicked grin, tossed her into a large incoming wave.

"This is war, mister!" she spluttered as she rose out of the wake. Lifting her arm high, she splashed him with all her might.

He smiled but narrowed his eyes before diving under water.

Having lost him, she pirouetted, searching for him. A steely grasp encircled one of her feet, yanking them out from her, and she was pulled under. Thinking quickly, she dragged in a breath before being submerged. She groped for him, hoping the strong hairy legs she found were her attacker's.

He grabbed her, gathering her close, and pressed his lips to hers. Gasping for air, they rose to the surface together. They bodysurfed, swam and stole a hundred kisses before finally turning back.

When they approached the spot where they'd left their stuff, they watched for a while to be sure no one awaited them.

"I think it'll be better if we split up. If they're still searching for us, they'll be looking for a couple, not singles. Meet me in the parking lot by the Jeep. I'll give you a head start. Go farther up shore in the water until you bypass our things before venturing onto the beach."

This all seemed too clandestine for a little make-out session. Yet it was fun, and just in case there was a problem, she went along with it. Thus several yards up shore, she ambled out of the surf, allowing her long hair to snarl over her face. Being nonchalant as she could, she didn't make eye contact with anyone.

The closer she got to the parking lot, the more her nerves started to thrum but she forced herself to go slowly as if she hadn't a care in the world. When she reached the Jeep, Harry sat inside waiting with the engine running.

He rolled down the window a few inches and ordered, "Hurry. Get in."

After she was ensconced in the vehicle and he had turned into traffic, he dragged in a long, ragged breath. "That was harrowing. I don't think I'm cut out for this exhibitionist stuff. Next time you want to do it in front of people, we'll go to a private club where we won't risk getting arrested."

Next time... A warm rush of feelings washed over her. He wanted there to be more. So did she.

Laying her hand on his thigh, she squeezed. "I want there to be a next time too, but you're more than enough for me."

A lazy smile dawned over his lips as he slid a warm glance at her. "Do you still want to look at cars?"

"I do, but let me check in at the hotel and make sure the coast is clear."

He quirked an eyebrow. "I thought you had the day off."

Grimacing, she said, "I'm always on call."

She pulled her phone out and checked for messages. Chantale had called several times but only left one voice message. "Call me. It's important."

What now?

"Excuse me for a sec. I need to find out what this is about." She dialed Chantale and waited for an answer. When the phone went to voicemail, she called the front desk and had her paged.

Finally, Chantale came to the phone. "Mademoiselle Lynette's been cooking again. José and his crew haven't been able to use the kitchen and we've had to close the restaurant. The guests are *très* unhappy."

Deanna wanted to pummel the cooking culprit but settled for slamming her hand on her leg. "Has anybody tried to get her to leave? Or, I don't know, asked her to join our staff and do her thing officially for us?"

Harry looked at her curiously and nudged her elbow. "What's going on?"

A raging headache approaching, she put her hand over the receiver and said, "Supposedly the ghost has hijacked the kitchen, thus we had to shut down the restaurant during lunch service. You got any bright ideas how to get a ghost in line?" The exorcism was sounding better and better.

Before he could say a word, however, she returned to Chantale. "We're on the way back. It'll take an hour or so, though. Meanwhile, are you sure you can't run the lunch service?"

"*Très* sure. Every time we try, knives start flying."

"She mustn't like our food." Somehow, aloud it didn't sound as funny as she'd intended. "Of course, no one can work in those conditions. Is it confined to the kitchen?"

"*Oui*, it's only in that one room. The bowling alley is still closed, as no one will work in there. If there's paranormal activity in there, it's quiet enough we've not noticed it."

"Keep an eye on it and don't let anyone enter that room. We will be there soon as we can. Have someone peek in the bowling alley and see if anything's going on in there as well."

"Will do."

She ended the call and tossed it in her bag. Reaching for her brush with one hand, she flipped open the mirror with the other and grimaced at her messy mane. She looked like the seaweed monster.

"Trouble in paradise?" Harry glanced at her with sympathy for a moment before he changed lanes to get around a slow-moving truck.

Fuming, Deanna brushed her hair so hard she pulled out several strands. Transferring her anger to him, she glowered in his direction. "Somebody is interfering with our kitchen service. Not only are they cooking up a storm, the knives are flying."

"Sounds like someone's angry. I wonder why?"

"Maybe she didn't like our séance. Maybe sister dearest has done something else to rile her up. Speaking of Roxanne, I've been doing some digging and I found that Davy Vandenburg died in the line of duty shortly after Lynette and Grant's demise." Harry pulled a few pages of computer printouts from the center console of his car, unfolded the bundle then handed them to her, all the while never taking his eyes off the road. "Look at these."

Deanna scanned the information quickly, not liking what she read but not at all surprised. "So our only hope to prove the murders is to get the corrupt chief of police to talk? Turn him against Roxanne? How easy will that be? Do you think Davy's death is suspicious?"

Harry nodded as he glanced in his rearview mirror before switching lanes. "I do. Very. The guy who shot him was never brought to justice. I'd be willing to bet Billy and Roxanne had something to do with it. They're still thick as thieves."

She chewed her bottom lip, thinking hard. "So how do we prove this? Do you have any brilliant ideas?"

"We get them to confess."

Surprised, she twisted in her seat to regard him and snapped her fingers high in the air. "Just that easy? And how do you propose we do that without getting ourselves killed?"

"Invite them to the next séance." Harry grinned as if he'd turned into Indiana Jones.

"*Next* séance? We're going to do it again? What makes you think they'll come?" She almost swallowed her tongue. One séance had been more than enough for her. She didn't know if she could stomach another.

"Like you, they don't believe in ghosts. They'll want to prove we're up to something."

"Or just kill us."

"There's that danger. We can have the security guards on hand for protection." He pulled into The Gilroy's parking lot and slid into a spot not too far from the door. Before getting out of the vehicle, he took Deanna's phone and flipped through the recent calls. Finally, he hit the redial with a somber, businesslike expression on his face.

"Roxanne Cambridge-Anderson, please." He was silent for a few moments, listening intently, deep lines etching in his forehead.

"No, this is Harry DeVeaux. I'm working with Deanna Thompson at The Gilroy. I want to invite you to a séance this evening." He held the phone away from his face and squinted. Then he added, "At five o'clock, sharp. We're going to summon your stepsister, Lynette Cambridge, and her fiancé."

Again, he paused, then he rolled his eyes. "No, I don't accept bribes. We're going to hold the séance with or without you. We're just giving you the courtesy of attending since it's about you and your good friend Billy Curtis."

When he poked the phone icon again, he did so with vicious force. "Bitch."

Curious as to what would bring on such a reaction, Deanna asked, "What did she say? Did she threaten you?"

Harry pinched the bridge of his nose between his fingers and heaved a loud sigh. "She's trying to bully us into stopping, warning us to stop talking to her stepsister — *or else.*"

"*Or else* what? She'll blow up your Jeep? Have us murdered?"

"She's too smart to be specific. She just said we'd be sorry if we don't drop this nonsense." He hopped out of the SUV and grabbed his change of clothes from the trunk before escorting her to her suite.

"Do you think it was smart to invite her? We know what she's capable of." The witch made their surly guests look like helpful little Boy Scouts. She looked up at her partner in crime with a mixture of apprehension and love.

Love? Tingles shot through her all the way to her toes. *Oh, my God. I've fallen in love with this man.*

How had she let this happen? Sure, he was handsomer than sin and the most charming man she'd ever met. And he was her hero, protecting her from reporters, surly guests and possible murderers. But he also cavorted with ghosts, tempted dangerous murderesses, and infuriated her! She must be crazy. Yet another realization hit her — she often angered him too, so they complemented each other.

Harry towered over her, his expression very serious. "We need to force a confession out of her. I don't know of any other way than to scare it out of her. I think it's past time she had a face-to-face with her sister."

Speaking low so the guests wouldn't hear her, she asked, "So you think Lynette will frighten her sufficiently that Roxanne will plead guilty?"

"It's usually the way we have to wring a confession from these bullies. You'd be surprised how fast criminals respond to homicidal ghosts."

Fright reverberated through her and she curled her fingers around his wrist. Tiptoeing up to him, she whispered, "Presuming there *are* killer ghosts, I'd be scared too."

He patted her hand and narrowed his gaze at her. "Trust me, there are. Stay close to me. Follow my lead and you'll be okay. These ghosts are out for Roxanne's and Billy's blood, not ours. We're their allies."

They hurried and showered. Once changed, Deanna into her hotel uniform and Harry into blue jeans and a white linen shirt, they sought out Chantale, who was guarding the restaurant entrance, making sure no one entered the danger zone.

"We're going to hold another séance at five. We'll perform it here in the kitchen," Harry said to Chantale, regarding her closely.

"I'll set it up." Chantale scurried away and arranged for a table and chairs to be brought in.

"Are we sure we want to set up near the knives?" Deanna eyed the sharp blades with trepidation.

"That's where the ghosts are so that's where we'll get our connection."

She wondered if Workman's Comp would pay if they were knifed in the middle of summoning ghosts. *Doubtful.*

Five o'clock arrived but Roxanne hadn't joined them. They were ready to start and Harry was the medium again. This time, they were just three, the minimum number required for the ceremony.

Chantale lit the candles as Deanna brought over a food offering and set it on the table, before she turned off the lights. Harry sat and beckoned the women to join him. Fortunately, the knives had stopped flying and Deanna could breathe easier.

"Let's hold hands very reverently," Harry instructed.

They gripped hands and looked at one another.

Harry spoke. "Lynette and Grant, we invite you to join us, to speak through us, to help us solve your murders. Please rap once if you will talk through me."

One long, loud rap sounded, then Harry began to chatter. "Welcome, spirits. Please tell us who is responsible for your deaths and how they murdered you."

The kitchen doors burst open and an older, well-dressed woman stomped in with Billy Curtis and some others. The woman with a blonde, frosted coif and tasteful gold jewelry in a three-piece emerald green power suit led the group. "Cease and desist!"

Blinking at the newcomers, Deanna did a double take and whispered, "Roxanne and Billy?"

"Better late than never." Harry glared at the tardy guests.

"Serve them with the desist order," Roxanne commanded of her minions. "Make them stop."

"What are you afraid of?" Deanna lifted her chin and glared at the woman who had threatened her. "Ghosts?"

"You're trying to frame me with this ghost nonsense. You're..."

"Roxanne. Billy. Long time no see." Harry stood and started speaking in a strange voice, his eyes glazed.

"I've never seen you before. We don't know each other." Roxanne crossed her eyes and looked down her long, patrician nose at Harry with thorough disgust. "Not unless you're trying to make believe you're channeling my stepsister."

"I am *not* Lynette, but you do know me." He turned to Billy and backed him into a corner. "You were my partner. I trusted you. Then you killed me to keep her sordid secret safe—for money. How could you trade my life for wealth and power?"

Deanna's head bobbed in the direction of whoever was speaking. She didn't think it was Lynette or Grant. Hurriedly, she turned on her cell phone video cam and started recording just in case the hotel's video cameras missed this. "Who are you?"

Harry turned dazed eyes on her, looking as if he didn't recognize her. "I don't know you, but I know them." He nodded at Roxanne and Billy.

"Who are you?" Chantale repeated the question with more authority.

Harry tilted his head and focused on Chantale. "Officer Davy Vandenburg. I was going to report my findings that Roxanne had shot and murdered Lynette Cambridge and Grant Haynes when Roxanne tried to pay me off to keep quiet. When I refused, Billy gunned me down, blamed it on our perps."

Roxanne put her hand to her throat. Her eyes feral, she pointed a shaky finger at Harry. "That's not true.

Davy died in the line of duty. It's all documented. He didn't die anywhere near this hotel. If Billy killed him, it had nothing to do with me."

Billy lunged at Roxanne, his hands going for her throat. "You bitch! It had *everything* to do with you! You killed your stepsister and her fiancé then paid me to kill Davy and cover it up. You're not going to throw me under the bus."

"He's right!" Chantale jumped up and faced Roxanne. "Your lackey killed Davy here in this hotel then moved the body to make it look like a murder in the line of duty. We witnessed the whole thing."

"Who are you?" Roxanne echoed Deanna's thoughts. The body may have been Chantale's but the voice, even the accent, was different.

"Don't you recognize me, dear stepsister? You're very well acquainted with the inheritance you stole from me."

Roxanne whipped around first toward Chantale, then Harry and finally Billy. "Billy, tell them you're lying, that you're under duress."

"I just told the truth, Roxanne, for the first time in forty years. You killed them. You wanted Lynette's money. You wanted her fiancé and you couldn't have either."

Butcher knives rose in the air, hovered for a few minutes then flew at Roxanne. With candlelight flickering eerily off their blades, the knives stopped an inch from her face.

Roxanne flinched and whimpered. She wrapped her arms around herself like a shield as her gaze darted from Billy to Harry, as she silently pleaded for help.

"Tell the truth, Roxanne. We're already dead, already in hell. It would give me great pleasure to do away with you the way you did with us."

"Then you can live together here in this hotel forever. Unless you go straight to Hell." Deanna couldn't stop herself from adding her two cents with an emphasis on the last part of her statement.

The knives twisted in the air and inched closer to Roxanne. When she tried to move away, more knives circled, holding her prisoner.

"Stop this! Put down the knives," Roxanne commanded, hugging herself. "This won't work. I'm not confessing to something I didn't do. Billy's insane. You can't believe a word he said."

"But you did it," Chantale said, circling the pair, looking them up and down. "I was there. I saw it. I'm tired of your lies, tired of watching you live out my life, tired of being stuck here."

When Roxanne pursed her lips, a specter of a woman flew out of Chantale with a loud, wild roar, and long, ragged teeth bared and aimed at Roxanne's neck.

Screams wrenched from Roxanne's throat and she ducked into a fetal position on the floor, covering her head with her arms. "Okay! I did it. I murdered you in cold blood. You had everything. I had nothing and you refused to share your wealth. My daddy raised you as his own, but you never treated me like a sister."

Deanna kept recording. "Say it again. Name names. Who did you murder? Explain in detail how you did it."

"I demand my rights. I want an attorney. I don't want to say another word without one."

The knives pressed closer, one drawing a drop of blood on Roxanne's neck.

"Spill, Roxanne. We don't give a damn about your rights just like you didn't give a damn about taking our lives." An iridescent, scowling Lynette hovered over her stepsister holding a butcher knife between Roxanne's eyes.

"All right! I'll confess if you stop bullying me, Lynette. When you refused to break up with Grant and sign over your inheritance, I went crazy. I shot you. Then I shot Grant. Billy helped me make it look like Grant shot you in a lover's rage then shot himself in remorse. You were the modern day Romeo and Juliet."

Harry sidled close to Deanna and looked to be himself once more. "Are you getting this?"

"Yes. All of it."

"Very good. Lynette, Grant and Davy should be able to move on after this. Your problems should be solved and you will no longer have a haunted hotel."

Roxanne sobbed and her makeup melted down her face in black rivulets. "Please make her stop, make her drop the knives. I've confessed. What more does she want?"

"Perhaps an apology would help," Deanna said, even though the fact that Harry would be leaving preoccupied her. After all, the case had been solved. Did that mean he'd walk out of her life too? Her heart flopping painfully, she started to close her eyes until she remembered she was still filming the confession.

Lynette's ghost shimmered and she floated in front of Roxanne, who cowered and scooted back. A moment later, a masculine ghost joined her and held her hand. They stood before Roxanne expectantly.

"Lynette. Grant. I was young and stupid and greedy. I deserve to be punished. I'm sorry. Please forgive me."

The ghosts gazed at one another and kissed. Then they looked back at Harry, Deanna, and Chantale and said, "Thank you." After that, they tilted their heads heavenward and soared through the ceiling.

Hugging herself, Chantale said, "That was beautiful. They have moved on. They are at peace."

Harry gathered Deanna into his arms and dropped a kiss on her head. "What do you think now? Do you believe in ghosts?"

A changed woman, Deanna nodded. "I believe. They were right in front of me. I mean, they were awesome. They got Roxanne and Billy to confess." She realized that Roxanne and Billy were sneaking away and she pointed at them. "Harry! They're trying to get away."

"Oh, no you don't!" Harry dove at Billy who pulled a gun and fired. The bullet whizzed past Harry, narrowly missing Deanna. It embedded in a pan hanging inches from Deanna's head.

"Stand back or I'll shoot to kill." Billy aimed the gun at Harry's chest.

Deanna's heart rose to her throat. "Harry, don't be a hero. Let him go."

"Give me your phone," Billy demanded, holding out his free hand.

As much as she wanted Roxanne and Billy to go to jail for their crimes, she wanted Harry and Chantale to be safe even more. She slid the phone across the floor toward Billy. Roxanne picked it up and pocketed it.

At that moment, Emily Spencer slammed in the door, her gun drawn, and Deanna slumped in relief. "Thank God you're here. They just confessed to murdering Lynette Cambridge, Grant Haynes, and Davy Vandenburg."

"I know what they did. I didn't know that they'd confessed." Emily clicked her tongue and turned the gun on Deanna. To Billy and Roxanne she said, "Go on. Get out of here. I'll hold them until you're clear."

Shocked, Deanna couldn't believe her ears. She looked at Emily with disgust. "You're the one working with them? Did you blow up my car and try to kill me or did they?"

"Does it matter? You had to come here and stick your nose where it didn't belong. I told you I didn't believe in ghosts. You said you didn't believe in them either, yet you insisted on hunting them down. You're as crazy as everyone else in this insane hotel. I can't take you people anymore."

"So you're helping murderers? *That* sounds crazy to me." Harry held up his hands but glared at the security guard. "What are you getting out of this?"

"I help them get away and I get set up for life in another country of my choice. Which one is none of your business. I don't need you tracking me down."

"So why not go? We're not stopping you. We're not a threat." Deanna stood and held up her hands too.

"Oh, but you are a threat. I think it's a shame this hotel will no longer be haunted. I think it should be. Since the former ghosts are gone, I think it needs new ones. You three know too much. Billy, help me eliminate them, will you?"

"It'll be my pleasure." Billy looked down the barrel of his gun and took aim at Harry while Emily set her sights on Deanna. Meanwhile, Roxanne walked out of the door, her head held regally high.

"Fuck this! Screw you!" Harry kicked the gun out of Billy's hand, ducked and rolled out of the way of the second gunshot that went astray.

Enraged and encouraged by Harry's bravery, Deanna took advantage of the moment when Emily was distracted and shoved the gun out of her hand. Chantale dove for the gun and picked it up.

Roger and two security guards rushed in.

Deanna yelled, "Take Emily Spencer and Billy Curtis into custody. They were going to shoot us."

As instructed, Roger apprehended the criminals and seized their firearms. "Are you okay? Are there any more?"

"Roxanne Cambridge-Anderson escaped. She's probably off the property by now. She took my phone with the evidence. Hopefully our video cameras got everything on tape."

Harry grabbed one of the security guards and said, "Come with me. Let's see if we can round up Roxanne." On his way out of the door, he called nine-one-one, summoning the police.

Minutes later, the police arrived and arrested Roxanne, Billy and Emily Spencer, hauling them away in a police cruiser. Roger, Deanna and Chantale reviewed the security tapes that showed everything. They made a copy for the police.

* * * *

After the excitement, Harry knocked on Deanna's door and hovered in her entryway. "That was, uh, some scene. Guess my work for The Gilroy is done."

"Another case well done. Right?" Deanna's heart was breaking. She didn't want to see Harry go. The place wouldn't be the same without him. *She* wouldn't be the same without him. "We'll be eternally grateful to you."

"Well, I wouldn't say that until you see our bill." Harry offered a lopsided, half-hearted grin as if he, too, wasn't completely happy.

"I'm sure your fee is well worth every penny. You saved our hotel and our lives. How can we ever repay you?"

Harry bowed gallantly in an exaggerated gesture. "Well shucks, ma'am, it was my pleasure rescuing such a beautiful damsel in distress."

She couldn't help but laugh. She almost fawned, fanned herself, and batted her eyelashes, and exclaimed, 'My hero', but held it back. Instead, she said, "Seriously, thank you. That was very brave of you, facing down a man with a loaded gun."

"I couldn't let anything happen to you. I swear I'd go nuts if I lost you." Sadness and something indiscernible flashed across his eyes.

Hope flared in her chest. Could he reciprocate her feelings? Were they in this thing together? She had to find out.

Taking a chance, she stood and closed the gap between them until there was only a hair's breadth separating them. Deanna gazed up at him, searching his eyes. "What do you mean? Do you care to elaborate?"

Her heart was pounding so loudly she was sure he heard it too. It was deafening to her. Or was she also hearing his heart?

For several long moments, he gazed down at her, a wealth of feelings in his irises. Then his thick lashes veiled his eyes and he dipped his head, capturing her lips. Against hers, he confessed, "Somewhere in the middle of all this, I fell deeply, madly, irrevocably in love with you. When your car exploded and I thought you might be dead, I went crazy. Then again today, when Billy and Emily threatened us, all I wanted to do was kill them to protect you. What about you? How do you feel about me?"

Awe struck her. He loved her. Deeply. Madly.

On tiptoe, she slashed a kiss across his beloved lips. "I love you, deeply, madly and irrevocably too. Even when I thought you were crazy to believe in ghosts, I couldn't help myself. You're the sexiest, kindest, most interesting man I've ever met. You have bewitched me. You're in my every waking thought. I want to be with you always."

"Do you still think I'm not in my right mind?" He stroked her hair back and tucked it behind her ears.

"Not at all. You're the sanest person I know." She burrowed against his heart, taking comfort in his arms.

"You said you like kids."

"What?" She lifted her face and frowned, wondering where he was going with this.

"I remember you saying that you like kids. You know, after the soccer team kids caused all that trouble. That you wouldn't mind having a couple of your own one day."

"Yeah. I said that. What about it?" She hoped she knew where he was going with this but kept her theories to herself.

"Will you marry me and have a couple of kids with me?" He circled her waist with his arms and rocked with her body tight against his chest.

"Will our children chase ghosts with you?" She nuzzled his chin with her nose, enjoying his slight, sexy stubble.

"Probably. Is that okay with you?"

"As long as I can help. Hotels are okay, but managing them takes too much time away from a family. Would you have room for me on your staff?"

"I think I could make room. That is, if you truly believe in ghosts. If you're not planning on becoming a full-time blogger or story writer."

Mention of her naughty blog brought heat to her cheeks. Although memory of it embarrassed her, she was glad she'd written the story. Otherwise, she and Harry might never have gotten together. She cleared her throat and shook her head. "Uh, I don't think you have any worries about me blogging so much that I'll ignore you. I have the real deal now. As per the ghosts, I've become a believer. Who wouldn't after a day like today?"

The events of the past several hours fast-forwarded in her mind. That included the hard time the hotel owners had been giving her since she'd arrived, so she truly didn't mind giving up her job. "I have to give at least a month's notice, however. It takes a while to find a decent manager.

"I don't know that I can wait that long. I'm used to being with you every day."

She winked and molded herself to him. Huskily, she said, "You, uh, could move in with me for now. What are they going to do? Fire me?"

About the Author

Ashley Ladd lives in South Florida with her husband, five children, and beloved pets. She loves the water, animals (especially cats), and playing on the computer.

She's been told she has a wicked sense of humour and often incorporates humour and adventure into her books. She also adores very spicy romance, which she weaves into her stories.

Ashley Ladd loves to hear from readers. You can find her contact information, website details and author profile page at http://www.totallybound.com.

Totally Bound Publishing